Room for One More

KAR-BEN
PUBLISHING

D1362912

Kar-Ben Publishing™
An imprint of Lerner Publishing Group
241 First Avenue North
Minneapolis, MN 55401 USA

Website address: www.karben.com

Image credits: stockcam/Getty Images (suitcase); wbritten/Getty Images (background).

Main body text set in Bembo Std Regular.
Typeface provided by Monotype Typography.

Library of Congress Cataloging-in-Publication Data

Names: Polak, Monique, author.
Title: Room for one more / by Monique Polak.
Description: Minneapolis : Kar-Ben, [2019] | Summary: In Montreal,
    Canada, in 1942, the war in Europe seems far off to fifteen-year-
    old Rosetta Wolff until her family takes in Isaac, a war refugee, and
    everything changes.
Identifiers: LCCN 2018045012 (print) | LCCN 2018051275 (ebook) |
    ISBN 9781541561267 (eb pdf) | ISBN 9781541540439 (pb : alk. paper)
Subjects: | CYAC: Family life—Canada—Fiction. | Brothers and
    sisters—Fiction. | Jews—Canada—Fiction. | Refugees—Fiction. |
    Antisemitism—Fiction. | Prejudices—Fiction. | Montréal (Québec)—
    History—20th century—Fiction. | Canada—History—20th century—
    Fiction.
Classification: LCC PZ7.P75226 (ebook) | LCC PZ7.P75226 Roo 2019
    (print) | DDC [Fic]—dc23

LC record available at https://lccn.loc.gov/2018045012

Manufactured in the United States of America
1-45248-36630-1/11/2019

For Sharon Browman, my fifth-grade
teacher and the first person to treat me
like a real writer—with love and gratitude
for introducing me to the real-life
Rosetta, who told me the
story that inspired this work of fiction

Chapter 1

I know it isn't right to listen in on other people's conversations.

But I can't resist.

My arms go goosebumpy with excitement when I am eavesdropping. It's the same feeling I get when I am making a speech.

I feel about eavesdropping the way my big sister, Annette, feels about new clothes. Or the way my little sister, Esther, feels about doing the long jump. It's how Mom feels about poetry and how Dad feels about Mom's Yorkshire pudding, the one she makes from Granny in England's recipe.

To me, nothing's so delicious as an interesting conversation.

The kind of conversation Mom and Dad are having tonight.

They have a guest—a man named Mr. Schwartzberg, whose dark, piercing eyes remind me of a fox's. He is small and thin and drags his leg behind him when he walks.

When Mr. Schwartzberg arrived, Dad and Mom called the three of us downstairs to shake his hand, but then they whisked him into the parlor and sent us upstairs with Anne-Marie, our housekeeper.

"Off you go, Andy, Ronald, and Eddie," Dad said, patting our heads.

Mr. Schwartzberg looked confused when Dad called us by boys' names. So Annette, who is sixteen and enjoys explaining things, explained: "It's because Dad wishes he had a son. If I'd been a boy, they'd have called me Andy, Rosetta would have been Ronald, and Esther, Eddie."

Mr. Schwartzberg nodded as if all this made perfect sense.

Dad objected, of course. "For the record, Mr. Schwarzberg, I want to state that on this August day in 1942, and for that matter, on every other day, I consider myself the luckiest man in all Montreal. Imagine living surrounded by so many talented, lovely females! My darling wife, Irene, devoted wife and mother, and part-time poetess; Annette, our resident *artiste* and fashion plate; Rosetta," (Dad smiled in my direction) "reigning public speaking champion of the grade-six class at Roslyn School; and Esther, our outstanding athlete."

Anne-Marie had trouble rounding us up for bed. "*Les filles!*" she said, clapping her hands. *Les filles* is French for "girls." Anne-Marie speaks to us mostly in English. But when she gets upset, she switches back to French, the language she was brought up with.

Annette and I were gossiping. She was critiquing Mr. Schwartzberg's clothing. "Has that man never heard of a tailor?" she whispered. "Those trousers are several sizes too large, and the jacket is unfashionably long."

"Are clothes all you ever think about?" I asked her. But because I knew that if Annette was angry with me, she'd never let me practice my speech in front of her, I added, "The new Eaton's catalog came in today's mail. I left it by your bed, open to the fall fashions."

"You did!" Annette squealed. "How wonderful! I can't wait to see it!"

Esther wanted to go outside to practice her long jump one more time. She also wanted her stuffed rabbit to watch her. Only then she realized she didn't know where she'd left him.

Anne-Marie shook her head and muttered, "This house has too many girls in it! *Il y a trop de filles!*"

"Well, you're one more girl!" Esther pointed out, which made all of us laugh, except Anne-Marie. Lately, Anne-Marie has been even more sour than usual. Mom says it's because Anne-Marie is worried sick about her big brother, Jean-Claude. He's part of Le Fusiliers Mont-Royal, and Anne-Marie's family has had no word of him since the Canadian troops raided the French port of Dieppe last week.

Maybe that's why when Anne-Marie brought Esther upstairs for her bath, she didn't notice when I snuck back downstairs.

Dad and Mom had shut the double doors behind them, which is how I knew they were going to have the sort of conversation we girls are not supposed to know about.

I slipped into the dining room and hid under Granny's table. Ever since the table, which is black mahogany and has been in Granny's family for generations, arrived, Mom has treated it like a new baby, inspecting it for scratches and warning us not to kick its legs when we're seated round it. Mom keeps the table covered with a linen cloth. The cloth has a long overhang, making it hard for anyone to tell when I am hiding underneath.

Since the dining room opens into the parlor, Granny's table is the perfect spot for eavesdropping.

I also come here sometimes for a little peace and quiet. There's a lot of giggling in a house with three sisters. Sometimes that makes it hard for me to think when I am in my room upstairs. I know I should be grateful that at least I have my own room. My friend Bertha Etkowitz has to share hers with her big sister Tova. I'd hate sharing a room with Annette. She is the moodiest person on Earth. Mom blames Annette's age. I just hope that when I turn sixteen, I won't catch whatever it is that Annette's got.

At first, the conversation in the parlor is about the weather. Dad asks Mr. Schwartzberg what he thinks of our Canadian climate. Mr. Schwartzberg has a thick accent, which makes it hard for me to understand him, but the longer I listen, the easier it gets. He explains that he hasn't yet experienced a Canadian winter, but that in Moravia, where he was born, the summers are as humid as the one we're having now. He admires our standing fan. There isn't one in the rooming house where he's staying.

When I peep out from behind the linen table-cloth, I see that Mr. Schwartzberg is looking around the room worriedly, as if he half expects someone to jump out and pounce on him at any moment.

"So you're staying at a rooming house, are you?" Dad asks.

Mom taps his arm. "Do you think there is some way, Martin dear, that we might be able to find a fan for Mr. Schwartzberg?"

"Let me see what I can do," Dad says.

"No, no, please no," Mr. Schwartzberg waves his hands in front of him. "That won't be necessary. Besides, I'm not planning to stay long in Montreal. I'm hoping to travel around Canada and also to the United States. You see I'm here on a mission."

"A mission," Dad says, a question in his voice.

I hear the clinking of the teapot. Mom must be checking to see whether the tea has steeped. "Would you like a little Earl Grey?" she asks Mr. Schwartzberg. "What about a maple scone? We've had to cut back on sugar on account of the new rationing system. Luckily, I managed to hold on to a few cans of maple syrup from last spring. We're all doing our part for the war effort." Mom lowers her voice when she says *war*. Ah-ha! So that's why Mom and Dad whisked Mr. Schwartzberg off the way they did, and also why he has such a thick accent. He's come to talk about the war in Europe.

Mr. Schwartzberg accepts the tea and a scone. He slurps his tea and then takes such a large bite of scone he almost chokes. A piece of scone comes flying out of his mouth and lands on the carpet, only an inch or so from my hiding place. I cover my mouth so I won't laugh out loud.

Mr. Schwartzberg reaches down to collect the piece of half-chewed scone. His face is very red. "Forgive me," he says, looking around the room again, and for a moment, I worry that like a fox sniffing for a goose, he has sensed my presence. Then he looks at Dad. "I've come to see you, sir," he says, "because I heard you are the treasurer of the oldest synagogue in Montreal. And that you are a good man. A decent man."

"I'm only the acting treasurer at the Spanish and Portuguese Synagogue. As for being a good man, I do my best. Now Mr. Schwartzberg, please tell us about this mission of yours."

Mr. Schwartzberg sucks in his breath, and I move closer to the edge of the table. I can tell he is getting to the interesting stuff. "Mr. and Mrs. Wolfson, I am sure you've heard that there are terrible things happening to Jews in Germany and Poland. And in other countries too. I've come to tell you more about these things, because I've witnessed them myself. Unspeakable things."

Mr. Schwartzberg sniffles, and I wonder if he's going to cry. I've never heard a man cry. What sorts of unspeakable things can Mr. Schwartzberg mean? I wish he'd hurry up and get back to his story!

"I'm so very sorry for what you must have been through," Mom says.

"Of course, I echo my wife's sentiments," Dad adds. "Now please, if it's not too difficult"—Dad hesitates for a moment—"tell us more."

Dad has a point. Telling all this is probably hard for Mr. Schwartzberg. I've been so interested in his story that I did not think about Mr. Schwartzberg's feelings.

I hear the teapot clink again. Mom must be pouring Mr. Schwartzberg more tea.

"I suppose you've heard of Hitler." Mr. Schwartzberg spits out the name.

"The German chancellor. Of course we've heard of him. We read the newspapers. We're doing all we can to support our brave boys overseas. May God be with them," Dad says.

I've seen photographs of this man Hitler in the *Gazette*. He has a short black moustache and a furious look in his eyes.

Mr. Schwartzberg clears his throat. "As you know, Hitler and his party—the National Socialists, or Nazis as they call themselves—blame all of Germany's troubles on the Jews. But that's not the worst of it. The Nazis have been singling Jews out, then rounding them up and transporting them to dreadful places. Places where Jews are treated like animals and worse."

Mom sucks in her breath.

I feel my shoulders getting tense. What does Mr. Schwartzberg mean when he says Jews are being treated worse than animals?

"How do you know these things?" Dad asks.

"I was on one of the transports. But I managed to escape. I jumped off a cattle car, which is how I injured my leg. My parents were too afraid to jump. And my brother," Mr. Schwartzberg sucks in his breath, "the Nazis shot him in the head while we were still in Moravia. He didn't line up quickly enough for their liking."

How could anyone shoot a man for not lining up quickly enough? It makes no sense! Why, it's the most awful thing I've ever heard.

Mr. Schwartzberg pauses to collect himself. "And so"—I can tell he needs all his courage to go on—"it has become my mission to let other Jews know the truth about what is happening overseas. So that you can find some way—any way—to help."

Chapter 2

"At my house, we have oatmeal for breakfast. Except on Sundays, when my dad makes pancakes. But did you know that in some parts of Italy, Italians eat dry cookies for breakfast, and they dip the cookies in red wine?"

I am standing at the end of my bed, trying to speak as clearly as possible and not bounce too much even though the mattress is making me wobble.

Glynnis, my best friend, is propped on the pillows, watching me. "You're going too quickly," she says. "And don't say Italians. If they live in Italy, it's obvious they're Italians."

I peek at my speech, which I have written out on a sheet of Hilroy paper. By next Tuesday, the day of our school's first public speaking competition of the year, I plan to know it by heart. It helps that

I'm fascinated by the foods people around the world eat for breakfast. Miss Vipond says it's important to choose subjects that fascinate us. "The audience," she says, "will sense your enthusiasm." Miss Vipond is my idol.

Glynnis is right. And I have to slow down. I speed up when I'm nervous.

"Do you think it's wrong to make a speech about breakfast when there's a war going on overseas?" I ask Glynnis. With every passing day, the *Gazette* has been reporting more casualties and deaths following the Dieppe raid. Thank goodness, Jean-Claude's name hasn't appeared on any of those lists!

I still haven't found the right moment to tell Glynnis about Mr. Schwartzberg and the conversation I overheard, though I haven't been able to get it out of my mind for even a minute.

"There's nothing wrong about it. We all eat breakfast—even when there is a war overseas. In fact, many people believe breakfast is the most important meal of the day. You should add that," Glynnis says.

"Would you hand me my pencil, please?" I ask Glynnis. I jot down what she just said and continue with my speech. "Egyptians eat fava beans for breakfast. They flavor the beans with lemon. In North

America, eggs with bacon is a popular breakfast meal. But because I'm Jewish, I don't eat bacon."

Glynnis's blue eyes flash. "That bit about being Jewish is off topic," she says. "Besides, there's no need to advertise your religion. You don't want to sound like Bertha Etkowitz, do you?"

I know Bertha from synagogue. She's come to play at my house a couple of times. Glynnis was not impressed. "Bertha is a horrible name," Glynnis had said when Bertha was out of earshot. "And why does she wear long sleeves on the hottest days of summer? Did you notice how all she talks about is being Jewish? I have never met anyone less fun in all my life."

I'm so glad to have Glynnis for my best friend that I don't dare defend Bertha. Besides, Glynnis is right; Bertha is a horrible name, she does talk a lot about Judaism, and no one could call her fun.

"I suppose mentioning my religion is off topic," I tell Glynnis. What I really want to say is that I hope she does not think there is anything wrong with being Jewish. Only Glynnis has a fiery temper and I don't want to set her off.

I scratch out the bit about being Jewish and clear my throat. "The British eat kippers for breakfast. In case you didn't know it, kippers are herrings that have been cut in two, salted, and smoked. They were one of Queen Victoria's favorites. A queen can have whatever she likes for breakfast, and she never has to do the dishes afterwards." Glynnis doesn't laugh at this part, though I hope the audience will find it funny.

"Was that business about Queen Victoria in the *Britannica*?" Glynnis asks. "Because if it was, Rosetta, you must bring in her photograph and pass it round the auditorium. You score extra points for visual aids."

Glynnis and I met when we were in third grade at Roslyn School. She was sitting in the desk behind mine, and we got in trouble for talking. For punishment, the teacher made us each write out the sentence, "I shall not speak out of turn," twenty-five times.

Besides being my best friend, Glynnis is my public speaking coach. She is perfect for the job because she has a talent for pointing out other people's faults. "I think you need to say something more when you go from bacon and eggs to kippers," she says now, her forehead wrinkled from thinking. "The ideas come too quickly in that section."

I've already rewritten this speech five times, but I want it to be the best it can be. How else can I expect to win another public speaking trophy at the end of grade six?

Glynnis lives just up Argyle Avenue, which means we can walk to and from school together every day. Argyle runs from Sherbrooke Street, which is the second-longest street in Montreal, up to the boulevard. Argyle is one of the prettiest streets in our neighborhood, which is called Westmount because it's west of Mount Royal, the small mountain after which Montreal is named.

Glynnis has one brother, Broderick. He's a year older than Annette and very handsome. Looking at him is like looking at the sun: so dazzling, it almost hurts. Glynnis has no sisters. That's why she likes coming here after school. "You're so lucky," she's always telling me, though sometimes she gets a headache from all the noise at my house.

Glynnis's eyes are cornflower blue, and she has a milky complexion and blonde hair that's mostly straight but with a perfect wave at the bottom. I wish I had Glynnis's hair. My own is mouse brown and curly, and never behaves the way I want it to. Sometimes, if Anne-Marie is in a good mood and caught up on all her chores, she irons it flat and I feel like a princess.

For now, we Montrealers can still iron when we want to; that isn't the case in Toronto. The *Gazette* says that as part of the action to support the war effort, Toronto housewives have been asked to stagger their ironing days to save electricity.

Annette and Esther are outside in our building. It was my idea to turn the wooden crate the dining room table came in into a building. At first, Mom worried it would spoil the lawn, but she changed her mind when she saw how much fun the three of us were having. Mom believes in Imagination. She thinks the word is so important that it should always be capitalized. I suppose that's because poetesses need Imagination the way teachers need blackboards or cooks need garlic.

From inside, Glynnis and I can hear the sounds of birds chirping and my sisters' laughter. "All right, get on with it!" Glynnis says, clapping her hands the way Miss Vipond does when she wants our class to settle down.

Glynnis checks her Timex—the one she got last Christmas. My speech has to be at least seven minutes long. If it's longer than eight, I'll be disqualified. Glynnis has promised that on competition day, she'll sit in the front row and give me a hand signal when my seven minutes are almost up.

I like making speeches because when I make one, everyone focuses on just me. When you have two sisters, that doesn't happen very often!

"I love your watch," I tell Glynnis when we finally take a break. We are sitting, cross-legged, on my bed.

"Don't you ever wish you had Christmas?" Glynnis's voice is gentler now that she's not critiquing my speech.

"Sometimes. But we have Hanukkah. It's a lovely holiday too."

"But you don't have a tree with a star on top and Santa doesn't come to deliver presents." I can tell Glynnis feels sorry for me. I don't like that.

"You don't really believe in Santa, do you?"

"No, not really," she admits.

"Besides," I say, "there are more important things than getting presents."

"Like what?"

"Well . . . like helping people who are in trouble."

Glynnis raises her blonde eyebrows. "What sort of trouble?"

"Mom and Dad had a visitor last week. A man named Mr. Schwartzberg." I drop my voice. I'm not sure whether what Mr. Schwartzberg told Mom and

Dad is supposed to be a secret. "I heard him say how European Jews are being badly mistreated."

"Were you eavesdropping again, Rosetta?" Glynnis wags her finger at me.

"I'm afraid I was. But honestly, Glynnis, I still can't believe what I heard. Mr. Schwartzberg said his brother was shot by the Nazis." Somehow, telling this to Glynnis makes me feel a little better.

Glynnis's pale skin gets even paler than when she was home with the flu and Mom sent me over with a pot of chicken soup. "Oh, my," Glynnis says. "How awful. Did Mr. Schwartzberg's brother do something wrong?"

I shake my head. "That's the worst part. He didn't do anything wrong. Unless you count being Jewish as something wrong."

Chapter 3

The blub, blub of the percolator and the clang of pots and pans wake me up. It's Sunday, which means Anne-Marie has the day off so she can go to Mass with her parents. Their whole congregation is praying for Jean-Claude. Anne-Marie and her family live in Saint-Henri. It's just down the hill from Westmount, though it feels like another world altogether. The houses there are teeny-tiny and cramped together, and they have hardly any yards at all.

Dad cooks on Sundays so Mom can get a day off too. Annette is helping with breakfast because although Dad is an excellent engineer who's good at building bridges, he gets flustered in the kitchen. Dad calls Annette his sous-chef, which means she hands him pots and peels potatoes.

"Andy!" I hear Dad shout, "Another fry pan! On the double!"

At least I get the bathroom to myself, without Annette rapping at the door, saying she needs to brush her teeth or put on eye pencil. Thank goodness Esther is too young to be vain. She isn't a morning person the way Annette and I both are. Esther is probably still in bed with her pillow over her head.

When we're all gathered round the dining room table, Esther still in her flannel nightgown, Dad clears his throat. "Boys, I should say girls," he says, winking at Mom. Then he looks at each of us in turn, a sign that what he is about to say is very important. "Mom and I have something to discuss with you."

"Don't tell me we're moving again!" Annette calls out. She is not good with change.

"Are we getting a dog or a kitten? I'd so love a kitten to snuggle with," Esther says in mid-yawn.

Dad pats Esther's head. "No, we're not moving and we're not getting a dog or a kitten. Though what we have to discuss with you this morning does involve an addition to our household."

"Mom and I were wondering," Dad says, "how you would feel about having a brother."

"Oh, Mom," Annette blurts out, "Are you pregnant again?"

Mom's cheeks redden like the stoplight at the corner of Sherbrooke Street and Victoria Avenue. "Now, Annette," she says.

Dad laughs. "No, it isn't that, my dear. This would be a ready-made brother."

I turn to Dad. "Ready-made? I've tasted ready-made sandwiches, but how in the world can a brother be ready-made?"

"I thought robins deliver babies," Esther says, looking confused.

Everyone laughs, except Annette. "You mean storks, not robins, silly," she says sharply.

I tousle Esther's hair. Esther likes to make us laugh, but she hates being called silly.

"This ready-made brother isn't exactly a baby," Mom says.

"What do you mean by 'isn't exactly'?" I call out.

"He's a young man," Dad says.

"How young?" I ask.

"He's Andy's age," Dad says. "Sixteen."

"Have you got a photograph of him?" Annette wants to know.

Dad raises his eyebrows. For a man who's almost

completely bald, he has surprisingly bushy eyebrows. "A photograph? Whatever for?"

"Well, if we're going to have a ready-made brother, it would be nice if he was handsome—tall and broad-shouldered, with almond-shaped eyes." It's clear from the dreamy look on Annette's face she is already picturing him.

I jab Annette with my elbow. "As if it makes any difference whether or not he is tall and broad-shouldered."

Annette jabs me back, only harder than I jabbed her. "Of course it matters," she says. "I'll have to look at him. So he'd better be handsome."

"What matters," Mom says, "is that this young man appears to have no family whatsoever. He's come all the way from Europe."

Esther shakes her head. "No family? How sad!"

"Where in the world are we going to put him?" I ask. It's not that I'm against our taking in an orphan—no matter what he looks like. I'm only being practical. As it is, there is only one bathtub for the five of us.

For a moment, the table falls silent—something that hardly ever happens at 442 Argyle Avenue. All I can hear is the sound of the grandfather clock ticking in the corner. *Tick, tock, tick.*

Mom and Dad exchange a look. I can tell they're deciding which of them is going to answer my question. In the end, it's Dad who does. "I'm afraid," he says, "we haven't planned that far. We thought that in the spirit of democracy, we should discuss the matter with you girls first. See how you felt about the idea."

"He could live in the building!" Esther suggests.

"Not in the winter, he couldn't," I tell her. "The building isn't heated."

"We'd have to rearrange the bedrooms," Mom says. "Annette and Rosetta, since you each have a large bedroom, Dad and I thought you two might bunk together."

Annette crosses her arms over her chest. "I'm not giving up my room. And I prefer not to share."

"Annette is very bad at sharing," Esther says.

"A person can get better at sharing," Dad says. I think he might mean me, too, and not only Annette.

"Does he play sports?" Esther asks. "We could play ball together. And what's his name? You haven't told us his name!"

"I don't know whether he is handsome or sporty. But I do know his name. It's Isaac. Isaac Guttman," Dad says.

"Isaac." I repeat the name as if it's part of a speech

I'm practicing. "Isaac Guttman." It's a name that fills your mouth when you say it.

Annette smooths her hair. Long, wavy, and black, it is her finest feature. "I'm still not keen on sharing with *her*," she says, glancing my way.

"What makes you think I'm keen on sharing with you?" I mutter under my breath.

"Girls!" Dad sounds stern. "I expect more from the two of you."

Mom strokes Dad's arm. "I'm sure they'll come around, dear. Now why don't you tell them about the coincidence?"

"Yes, yes, I nearly forgot. The coincidence." Dad's face relaxes. "Well, I saw this young man's name on a list that was circulated by the Canadian Jewish Congress. Isaac Guttman. Isaac Guttman." For a moment, Dad closes his eyes. "There was something familiar about the name. And then it came to me: my mother, your granny, helped to support a young war refugee named Isaac Guttman when he was living in England. The boy was born in Düsseldorf, Germany. I made some inquiries, and imagine this—it's the very same fellow. So he already has a connection to our family. I think your granny would be very pleased if we took him in."

Though I've only met her twice in all my life, I adore Granny in England. She's regal and well read, and she writes the most interesting letters. I want to please Granny, but I'm still not convinced we should let this boy come and live with us. And I really don't want to share a room with Annette!

"Where is Isaac? Is he outside now?" Esther asks as if she expects him to be delivered by the truck that brought us Granny's table.

Mom and Dad exchange another look. I can see they are deciding how much to tell us. My ears prick up the way they do when I'm eavesdropping.

Dad clears his throat. "He's in an internment camp on St. Helen's Island, in the St. Lawrence River," Dad says. "He's been there for nearly a year."

"What's an in-ter . . . camp?" Esther asks.

Annette sighs. "It's a kind of prison."

Mom bites down on her lower lip. I think she wishes Annette had not been so direct. "It *is* a little like a prison," Mom tells Esther. "But not quite as bad."

Dad picks up the explanation. "I've heard there are four hundred men living together at the internment camp," he says. "They're forced to do hard labor, like chopping down trees, and are paid very little for it. Most of the men are Italian or German, and rumor has it they aren't too kind to the Jews. It can't be easy for a boy like Isaac—to be on his own in a place like that, without family of any kind."

"Poor Isaac!" Esther crosses her hands over her heart. "We must let him come to stay!"

"That is what Mom and I think too. But since all of you will be affected by this change in our living arrangements, I think it's best to take the matter to a vote. A show of hands if you please."

Three hands shoot up into the air. Dad's, Mom's and Esther's. After a few moments' hesitation, Annette raises her hand too. I look around the table. Even if this young man has had a hard time, even if he is a friend of Granny's, where is he going to sit? We don't have enough chairs!

But the others are looking at me, and so, in the end, I raise my hand too, though not as high as everyone else's.

Chapter 4

"My parents say they'd never do it. In fact, my mother says it's a spectacularly bad idea—letting a strange boy move into a house full of girls."

I can just imagine Glynnis's mother saying that. Mrs. Benbow is a terrible worrier, always fussing over Glynnis and reminding us to look both ways when we cross Argyle Avenue—as if we're five, not twelve!

"To be honest," I tell Glynnis, "I'm not that keen about the idea myself. But Granny knows the boy. She paid for his room and board when he was living in England, and she had him over several times for Shabbos dinner. She'd never have befriended him if he had a bad character. Besides, it's the right thing to do. Imagine cutting down trees all day, being treated unkindly because you are a Jew, and not having a family to support you. Do you think he and Broderick might become friends?"

I try not to give anything away when I say Broderick's name. I don't want Glynnis to know how handsome I think her brother is. She'd tease me. Or worse, she'd tell him.

"You never know with Broderick," Glynnis says.

We are trudging up Argyle. We stop to admire a mountain ash tree. Usually, it's just a plain-looking tree with a thick trunk and green leaves. But for a week or two every September, the mountain ash bears bright orange berries. Though the berries aren't for eating, they are awfully pretty.

Today is the first round of this year's public speaking competition, and my heart thumps a little harder as we approach the front doors of our school. I slept the whole night with my speech under my pillow. It's a trick I use for memorizing.

"When is this Isaac arriving anyhow?" Glynnis asks.

"This coming Sunday. Do you think Broderick might want to come and meet him?"

"Maybe. Though only after Isaac has had a proper bath. Mother says he's likely to be crawling with lice."

I scratch behind my ear. Even if I'm still not entirely in favor of Isaac moving into our house, I don't like Glynnis or her mother speaking badly about him.

Miss Vipond is sitting at the back of the auditorium, looking as elegant as always. Her chestnut hair is wrapped in a bun. She is wearing her pearl choker and her back is stick straight. Miss Vipond says that a straight back makes the brain work better and that if we don't pay attention to our posture when we're young, we could end up like the hunchback of Notre-Dame.

Miss Vipond nods when I take my place at the podium. I reach into my blazer pocket for my speech. My fingers tremble. I hope I won't drop the paper.

I try to remember everything Miss Vipond taught us. Look at the back of the room. That makes everyone think you are speaking directly to them. Smile, though not too much. Never race through your speech. And finally, breathe. Let the air enter through your diaphragm, feel your lungs fill up, and then exhale out.

The sheet my speech is on is folded into four. I know it by heart, thanks to the pillow trick. The judges will be impressed if I can manage without reading off the sheet. For a moment, I picture myself after the next round of competition, holding another silver trophy cup. I can practically feel its weight in my arms and see my name, Rosetta Wolfson, engraved on it.

My eyes land on Glynnis. She is sitting in the front row, looking businesslike, her Timex laid out on her lap. The auditorium feels suddenly too warm, so I shake off my blazer and leave it behind the podium.

"Ladies and gentlemen, fellow students," I begin. I take a deep breath, exactly as Miss Vipond said. I step away from the podium and turn a little to the side. When I do, I notice that Glynnis is flapping one arm. Why is she doing that?

I look over at Miss Vipond. Her eyes are very big. I haven't properly begun my speech, and yet both Miss Vipond and Glynnis are making me think something is wrong. What could it be?

Gerald O'Shaughnessy, whose turn is after mine, smirks at me from the side of the auditorium, where the other contestants are sitting, lined up in a long row of wooden chairs. Is it my imagination, or are some of the others smirking too?

I look down at the stage floor, and that's when I

realize it—something is hanging like a tail from the back of my tunic.

Oh my God, I have never been so embarrassed in all my life!

It's a pair of Mom's underpants!

They must have gotten caught inside my blazer, probably when Anne-Marie was taking in the laundry from the clothesline. Then when I took off the blazer, the underpants must have gotten stuck to the back of my tunic!

No wonder Glynnis is flapping her arm and the others are smirking!

I reach down for the underpants and swoop them up. My cheeks are on fire. I take the underpants and stuff them behind the podium, underneath my blazer.

Someone cackles—Gerald O'Shaughnessy?—and someone else at the back of the room, a teacher probably, shushes him.

I clear my throat. Only now, I can't remember what I'm supposed to say. My mouth opens, but no sounds come out. All I can think of is those underpants.

I'm hoping the words will come to me by magic, but they don't. I look at Glynnis. Her eyes are flashing. She looks angry. But what I see in Miss Vipond's eyes is even worse. Miss Vipond is sorry for me. When she catches me looking at her, she gives me a tight-lipped smile.

I unfold my speech and lay it out on the podium with trembling fingers. I have no choice now but to read it. I already know I have lost today's competition.

Every pair of eyes in the auditorium is watching me.

"At my house, we have oatmeal for breakfast . . ." I read from the unfolded sheet.

"Is that before or after you put on fresh undies?" a voice calls from the audience. This time, I know for sure it's Gerald. Others are giggling now, too, and more teachers are saying shush.

"Except on Sundays, when my dad makes pancakes. But did you know that in some parts of Italy, Italians eat dry cookies for breakfast, and they dip the cookies in red wine?"

I'm going too quickly, but I can't slow down and I can't catch my breath. I'm a stallion galloping too quickly. My fingers, my knees, my ankles . . . every part of me is shaking.

In all my life, this is the worst thing that has ever happened to me. How will I ever recover?

Chapter 5

It's decided. Annette and I will share a room. Neither of us is too thrilled about it. I'm the one who has to give up my room; Annette, who is very fussy about her things, will have to share hers. She has already hung a piece of butcher's string down the middle of the room to mark which side is hers.

"And don't go touching my clothes," she warns. I think Annette could be a little more welcoming. After all, I'm the one who has to give up my room altogether. But I don't say anything. We're all a little afraid of Annette.

Anne-Marie isn't too happy either. "What if he's messy?" she mutters as she shines the windows with sheets of newspaper she has dipped in a vinegar solution. "What if his feet stink? What if he gobbles up all the groceries the way young men do? Jean-Claude used to eat half a loaf of bread every day," Anne-Marie says, wiping at her cheeks when she mentions Jean-Claude.

Esther comes inside with a bouquet of purple asters. "I picked them," she says, pressing the flowers to her chest, "for Isaac."

Even Mom, who is very proud of her asters and who would probably rather see them in the garden than wilting in the house, is touched by Esther's kindness. "I'm sure Isaac will be delighted, dear. Now let's see if we can find the right vase to show off those flowers."

In the end, Isaac is not delivered by the Meldrum truck that brought us Granny's furniture. He is coming by train, and Dad has gone to get him at Windsor Station. It seems right that Isaac is arriving on the second day of Rosh Hashanah, the Jewish New Year. Because it's a High Holy Day, Dad can't take the car. He and Isaac are going to walk from the station. Dad will hire a cab to bring Isaac's bags.

"I think it's best I go alone," Dad told us when we said we wanted to come. "Isaac isn't used to ladies, and I'm afraid the beauteous sight of all three of you when he's just stepping off a train might do him in. The poor fellow might faint! Besides, you can help Mom and Anne-Marie with the preparations for Rosh Hashanah lunch. Someone has to slice the apples and pour the honey!"

"And don't go asking Isaac about the war or about that dreadful man Hitler," Mom warns us. "The poor boy has been through a lot, and we must give him time." Mom turns to me. "Rosetta, is that clear? I know how much you like asking questions."

"I'll give him time. I promise," I tell her. Inside, though, I am hoping Isaac will not take too long to warm up and tell me everything about himself.

The table is set with Mom's best china. Before he left for the station, Dad brought up an extra chair from the basement. We've prepared two plates with apples and honey to welcome in what we hope will be a sweet new year and our new brother. Once all that is done, Mom decides we should wait with her in the front parlor. "They should be arriving any minute," she says, glancing up at the grandfather clock. "Esther, one of your ringlets is covering your left eye."

"These socks make my legs scratchy." Esther is always getting rashes or dry skin.

"Let me see," Mom tells her, "and by the way, pet, you mean itchy. Scratch is what we do to fix an itch."

We hear Dad's voice from the front yard. "Well then, Isaac, here we are. Welcome to 442 Argyle Avenue."

Annette and I race to the front window and jostle each other to get the best view. "Now, girls, stay calm," Mom tells us.

Esther presses herself in behind us. "Does he look sporty?" she asks. "And is he really going to faint?"

"Of course not," Annette says. "Dad was only joking when he said that."

I press my face against the windowpane. I can't tell yet what he's like. Only that he's tall and gangly.

"Girls!" This time, Mom sounds very stern. "Get away from that window this instant. I won't have you gawking!"

The doorbell rings. "We've arrived!" Dad calls out. "Come and meet your new brother!"

The three of us rush to the front door. Of course, Esther gets there first. "I'll answer," Mom says, shooing her away. "The rest of you will meet Isaac in a moment. And remember," she drops her voice, "don't overwhelm the boy. He isn't used to female company. And no mention whatsoever of the war in Europe."

A moment later, there is Isaac on our front step, peeping out from behind Dad's back. Isaac takes a step forward so he is standing next to Dad on the welcome mat. So this is Isaac Guttman. Our ready-made brother.

He's not handsome.

But he isn't ugly.

He is somewhere in between.

He has sandy-colored hair, a sharp nose, high cheekbones, and dark nervous eyes that remind me of Mr. Schwartzberg's. There's something else about those eyes—as if he is sizing us up. He is not tall or broad-shouldered; his hair lacks shine. If he were a tree, he'd be scrawny birch, not a majestic oak. Miss Vipond would not be impressed by Isaac's posture. His shoulders slope like an old man's. He turns away when he catches me looking at him looking at us. No, I decide, he's not the sort of brother I hoped for.

"Isaac, my dear," Mom says, extending her hand. "We're delighted that you've arrived."

Isaac shakes Mom's hand. His fingers are thin and chapped, probably from chopping wood. I see veins poking through from underneath the skin on the back of his hand.

Esther pulls on the hem of Mom's dress. "Annette isn't delighted." Though Esther is whispering, it's still loud enough for all of us, including Isaac, to hear. "And neither is Rosetta," Esther continues. "The two of them will have to share Annette's room. Annette is bad at sharing. And Rosetta snoops."

"Esther!" Mom spins round to face her. "Hush now, will you?"

Isaac is still standing in the doorway, but now he looks a little frozen, as if he isn't sure whether he really wants to come inside.

Just then, a cab pulls up in front of the house. The driver pops out. He makes a single trip because Isaac only has one bag: a scuffed-up brown leather suitcase with worn canvas straps and rusty buckles. Imagine all of one's things fitting in just one case!

"Are you coming in or not?" Annette asks Isaac, tapping her foot on the parquet floor. "You can't just stand there all day. I don't know about you, but the rest of us are starving."

"Yes, yes, I'm coming *een*," says Isaac. When I imagined a ready-made brother, I didn't expect an accent, though of course, I should have.

"I picked these for you," Esther says from behind her bouquet of asters.

Isaac takes the flowers and looks at all of us. "I'm *over-velmed*, just *over-velmed* by your generos—" Isaac lets out a sneeze. I wonder if he has a cold or if he is allergic to flowers.

"Bless you!" we all say at once.

When Isaac uses his jacket sleeve to wipe his nose, Mom bristles and Annette's eyes get big.

"You are all so kind," Isaac says. "And I'm sorry that the two of you"—he turns to Annette and me—"have to share a room because of me."

"We're glad to do it." For someone telling a bold-faced lie, Annette sounds surprisingly convincing.

Anne-Marie is supervising from outside the kitchen door. Just as Isaac is about to walk inside, she calls out, "Your shoes!"

"*Vhy*, yes, of course." Isaac leans down to unlace his shoes and adds them to the row of shoes already parked in the hallway. He is wearing thick khaki-colored socks. I can't help noticing that both heels have been coarsely darned.

Anne-Marie wrinkles up her nose. I'd have thought she'd be relieved that Isaac has removed his shoes (she hates when we track dirt inside the house), but then I remember she was worried his feet might stink. I sniff the air discreetly. No stink.

Esther is following at Isaac's heels the way a puppy might. "You talk funny," she says.

"Esther!" Mom says. "Mind your manners!"

Isaac blushes. "I know I do. I'm sorry."

"There's nothing to be sorry about," Dad says.

Isaac kneels on the carpet so he is at eye level with Esther. "Maybe you can help me *viss* my elocution."

"Elo— what in the world is that?" Esther asks, giggling.

"I'll help you with your elocution." Annette says in her bossy way.

"Do you play ball?" Esther asks.

"I certainly do. I also like to sprint. Like you."

This news makes Esther grin.

Isaac turns to me. "You must be Rosetta, the public speaking champion." Instead of feeling proud when Isaac says that, I am suddenly reminded of my recent disaster. The memory makes me blush.

How does he know so much about us?

Dad shows Isaac the front closet where he can hang his jacket. Annette and I look at each other. I think we are both hoping he won't put his snotty sleeve too close to our coats.

Mom is holding onto Dad's elbow, her face glowing. Maybe Dad isn't the only one who hoped for a son.

Chapter 6

Of course we fight. How could three sisters living in a house with only one bathroom never fight? It's just that since Isaac arrived, we're fighting more and the fights are worse.

The first one starts with a squabble, the way many fights do. Dad asks which one of us wants to give Isaac a tour of the house before Rosh Hashanah lunch. "I do!" the three of us say at the same time. I even raise my hand because that's what I do in school when I want Miss Vipond to pick me to conjugate a Latin verb.

"I'm the eldest," Annette says, "so I'll do it."

"Just because you're the eldest doesn't mean you should always get your way. I'm the one who had to give up my room." I chew on my lower lip. I shouldn't have blurted that out. Not with Isaac standing so close by.

That's when the squabble beomes a fight. It's like watching the fireplace for the moment when an orange ember catches and bursts into flame. "I wouldn't mind sharing so much," Annette hisses, "if you were more respectful of my things. Even Anne-Marie can't get the tea stain out of my gray flannel skirt—the one you borrowed without asking first."

"You'd never have let me wear it!" I say. "Besides, it's too small for you!"

"It is not too small for me," Annette says, stamping her foot.

"All you ever think about is clothes!" I tell her.

"That isn't true, and you know it!"

"Well, then, name one other thing you think about!"

"Now, now, girls!" Mom says, straightening her back the way she does when she is upset. "Stop it! This is no way to behave around your new brother."

"I'm sorry," I say, speaking more to the parquet floor than to Isaac.

Annette doesn't bother to apologize, even though what she's said to me is as bad as what I said to her.

She grabs Isaac's arm. "Well, then, it's settled. I'll give you the tour. It isn't a very large house, so it won't take long. By the way, Isaac, if you need to blow your nose, just tell me so and I'll find you a proper handkerchief."

"Can I show him our building?" Esther asks, tugging on Isaac's shirttails.

★ ★ ★

We're all on our best behavior over Rosh Hashanah lunch. Isaac does not have to blow his nose. Mom looks pleased when he compliments her challah bread. Dad makes a toast to the New Year and to our new brother. No one mentions Hitler or the war in Europe. Esther introduces Isaac to her stuffed rabbit and giggles happily when Isaac shakes one of the rabbit's paws. After dessert, she gets up from the table to demonstrate her long jump.

The second fight starts after we've cleared the dishes. It's about who will help Dad carry Isaac's heavy case upstairs. Esther and I both want to do it. Annette says there are a few spots she and Isaac missed on their grand tour.

I can feel Isaac half watching us from the dining room, where Annette is showing him the portrait of Mom's parents. "Please," he calls out, his dark eyes darting between the portrait and the rest of us, "I can carry my own case."

"We wouldn't hear of it," Dad tells him. "Ronald," Dad says to me, "grab that end."

"Why do I never get picked to help?" Esther asks. "It isn't fair. I hate being the youngest."

"Move!" I tell Esther. "You could get crushed."

"I don't care!" Esther says.

"Eddie!" Dad uses his sternest voice, and Esther moves out of the way.

Dad and I lug the heavy case upstairs. "Martin," Mom calls from the landing, "I hope you aren't straining your back, darling!"

Dad and I deposit the case at the foot of my—I should say Isaac's—bed. Mom has replaced my pink quilt with a bedspread that is dark green and more for a boy.

I've only shared a room with Annette for a few days, but I already miss my own bed—and my privacy.

"Ronald," Dad says, "let's get it a little closer to the window." As I help Dad, I think of all the faraway places this case has been. Isaac has lived in Germany and then, for nearly two years, in England, not far from Granny's home in Hove. Then, when the British government decided to get rid of what it called enemy aliens, Isaac and his case were sent to the internment camp on St. Helen's Island, here in Montreal. If the case could speak, I wonder what stories it might tell.

Opening the case is my idea. By then, Dad has gone to his and Mom's bedroom to stretch out his back. Mom is behind him, making clucking sounds and saying how she told him so.

"Let's open it!" I say to Esther, who seems to have forgotten that she was upset five minutes ago. "That way we can put away Isaac's things before he comes upstairs."

The truth is I am mostly interested in knowing what's inside his case.

Esther and I squat down in front of the case. I unlatch the buckles, and together, we hoist the thing open. It smells mustier than our cellar.

"What are you two up to?" It's Mom. She is standing in the hallway, looking stern, her hands on her hips. Mom doesn't usually raise her voice.

Now Dad comes rushing down the hall. He is pressing his hand against the small of his back.

"What in God's name is going on now?" he asks.

"They're going through Isaac's things!" Mom tells him.

But I am too interested in what's inside the case to worry about Mom and Dad. On top is a frayed photograph in a tarnished silver frame. The photograph is of a dark-haired heavyset woman with black eyes and a serious expression; she must be Isaac's Mom. Except for the eyes, they don't look much alike.

Underneath are three cardboard boxes, their edges reinforced with packing tape. Now I see the word "BRIEFMARKEN" inscribed in bold, black letters on the first box. Because I'm curious to know what *Briefmarken* means, I pull the lid off. The box is filled with stamps! Dad, who collects stamps too and is always saying how he wishes one of us would share his passion, will be thrilled. "Dad," I call out, "Isaac has brought stamps with him from across the ocean!"

Annette and Isaac have also come upstairs. Isaac eyes the box that I have opened, and the two unopened boxes next to it. I cannot tell from his face whether he minds that we have opened his case and discovered his stamp collection. In fact, I cannot tell a thing from Isaac's face—it has gone perfectly blank. Miss Vipond would call Isaac's face a tabula rasa, an empty slate.

"Please forgive Rosetta and Esther," Mom says to Isaac, "they should never have gone ahead and opened your case."

"We were only trying to help," I say. "We thought you'd feel more comfortable if we put out some of your things."

Isaac's face still looks as blank as the Sphinx's in the old story. It's only when Esther picks up the tarnished frame that something in Isaac's face changes. His Adam's apple jiggles, and the skin on his cheeks gets tight.

"Would you like this photo on your night table?" Esther asks. "So you can keep your mom close."

The tension in Isaac's cheeks moves up to his dark eyes. He blinks, but only for a second; when the blink is over, his face is as blank as before. "That's not my mom," is all he says.

Chapter 7

Because yesterday was Yom Kippur, the holiest day of the year for Jewish people, I didn't go to school. Instead, I fasted (which wasn't easy) and went to shul with Dad, Annette, and Isaac. I think Isaac came because he had to. Though now that I think about it, that's probably also why I go to shul.

Shul is never so busy as on Yom Kippur. That's because everyone has sins to atone for. Mine are being snoopy and too focused on my own feelings. And maybe snapping at Annette, even though she deserves it.

"You seem to be paying more attention to Mrs. Etkowitz's hat than you are to the rabbi's sermon," I told Annette during the service.

To be honest, it would have been difficult *not* to pay attention to Mrs. Etkowitz's hat, which had blue and orange feathers glued to the rim.

Bertha saved for a seat me in shul. "Oh, Rosetta," she said, grabbing my elbow, "how I've missed you here at synagogue. I come every single Saturday. Is that your new brother, Isaac? He has a wonderful name. Did you know the biblical Isaac was nearly sacrificed by his father, Abraham? Until an angel intervened. Perhaps you are Isaac's angel."

"*Me*—an angel? I don't think so!"

"Rosetta! How can you make jokes on this holiest of holy days?" Bertha asked. Her tone was serious, but I could see from her eyes she was trying not to laugh. For a moment, I felt sorry for not trying harder to be better friends with her.

By sunset, I was so hungry I could have eaten a horse. Mom warned Annette and me (Esther is too young to fast) not to complain in front of Isaac. "God only knows what that boy has been through," Mom said.

Isaac does seem to be enjoying Mom and Anne-Marie's cooking. Though he's only been with us for a week, his face is filling out. He fasted yesterday, too, though he didn't complain the way Annette and I did.

This afternoon, I'm at the dining room table, working on my Latin verbs. Dad and Isaac are at the other end of the table, hunched over Dad's stamp collection. Isaac has brought his cardboard box downstairs. He has thousands of stamps, all organized by country. Most are from Germany, but some are from as far away as Barbados and a country called Madagascar. One stamp from Madagascar has two orange butterflies on it. That's Esther's favorite.

"Pass me the loupe, Isaac, if you don't mind," Dad says so he can take a closer look at the stamp.

The magnifying loupe is Mom's. She needs it to read and also when she's writing. Mom's eyes are getting worse by the day. She says it's part of growing old. But Dad is five years older than Mom and his eyes are fine. He only uses the loupe when he's working on his stamps.

Dad and Isaac are examining a reddish-colored stamp with a picture of the famous German composer Johann Sebastian Bach on it. The postmark is from 1936. "This stamp is in excellent condition," Dad says to Isaac. "It has no tears, and the corners aren't bent."

Isaac looks pleased. Some of his stamps are in *mint condition*, which means they were never used. I'm more interested in the ones that have traveled places.

Because it's a warm afternoon, Esther is playing in the building. Mom is busy in the kitchen with Anne-Marie, packing sandwiches for our picnic at Beaver Lake in Mount Royal Park. Beaver Lake is the best picnic spot in Montreal. The lake, which is shaped like a four-leaf clover, used to be a swamp with beavers in it! In warm weather, families picnic in the grassy area overlooking the lake. In winter, the lake is perfect for skating on.

"I can't tell you, Isaac," Dad says, "what a treat it is to finally have someone in the household who shares my interest in stamps."

I feel a pang in my chest when Dad says that. For the first time since Isaac arrived, I feel a little jealous of him.

"If you don't mind my asking," Dad says to Isaac, "how is it you developed an interest in stamp collecting?" It's the most personal question Dad has asked Isaac since he came to live with us.

I peek out over the top of my Latin textbook. There are so many things I'd like to know about Isaac's past. If she isn't his mom, then who is the dark-haired woman in the photograph by his bedside? What sorts of terrible things did Isaac see in

Europe? Glynnis thinks he might even have laid eyes on Hitler himself.

Isaac shuts his eyes. I've noticed he does that when he's thinking—or like now, remembering. "Stamps are little works of art," he tells Dad. "But to be honest, my interest grew out of practical concerns."

"What do you mean by practical concerns?" Dad asks.

"*Vee* couldn't bring more than ten marks *viss* us when we left Germany on the Kindertransport. But the Nazis had no interest in stamps. Then, when I arrived in England, I was able to trade my stamps with other collectors. To make a little—how do you say it?—pocket money."

I've never heard the word Kindertransport. It must be some sort of transportation having to do with children, like in the word *kindergarten*. But now, at least, I know how Isaac escaped from Germany.

"Most impressive," Dad says, nodding his head. Because Dad is studying another stamp, it's hard to know whether he is more impressed by Isaac's stamp collection or by his instinct for business. Either way, I can't help wishing Dad would be a little less impressed with Isaac altogether.

Annette never just enters a room; she bursts in, like Mount Vesuvius erupting. Vesuvius is wearing a new dress. It's navy blue with white piping. Because Annette is the eldest, she's the only one who gets new dresses. Esther and I have to settle for hand-me-downs.

Annette has noticed me noticing the dress. "Do you like it?" Her voice is so sweet I know for sure she's teasing me.

"Take good care of it," I tell her. "After all, in four years it'll be mine."

"Well, then, one of us had better take good care of it. And we all know it won't be you, Rosetta!"

Just then, Mom comes into the dining room with her hands on her hips. "Our picnic lunch is ready," she announces. "If you two gentlemen could take a break from admiring stamps and carry the picnic basket out to the car, I'd be much obliged. Rosetta, dear, can you try to tear your sister away from that building of hers? Tell her I've made her favorite— egg salad with gherkin pickles."

Isaac gathers his stamps from the table and returns them to their box. "I'm nearly done, 'sir'," he tells Dad, who's getting up from his chair.

Dad turns to Isaac. "There's no need to call me sir."

Isaac's cheeks turn pink. "Oh, of course not. But then what should I call you, sir . . . oh, excuse me, please. I said it again."

Father rubs his chin. "You could try calling me 'Dad' the way my girls do."

My heart catches when Dad says that. After all, he is *our* dad, not Isaac's. But then I tell myself Dad could never love this strange boy as much as he loves us—even if Isaac shares his passion for stamp collecting.

"Yes, sir, I mean Dad." Isaac's right hand tenses up and for a moment, I think he's going to salute Dad. "I'll do my best, s—" Isaac catches himself, "Dad."

Mom leads the two of them into the kitchen to show them where the picnic basket is.

Annette goes upstairs to use the bathroom. I head outside to collect my little sister.

When I step into the building, I hear cooing. Is there a pigeon in here? Then I spot Esther lying on the floor. She's playing hospital. It is one of her favorite games.

"Playtime's over, Esther! We're going for a picnic. Mom made egg salad sandwi—"

Esther lifts her head, but then she lets it drop back down. Esther is very good at pretending to be the patient. "All right," I tell her. "I'll play hospital with you. But only for a minute. Good day, Madam," I say in my best imitation of a doctor. "You seem a little unwell today. I'd better take your temperature."

When I press my hand to Esther's forehead, it feels hotter than our radiators in the dead of winter. Has she been practicing her jumps?

Usually Esther starts to giggle when I pretend to examine her. It's the fact that she isn't laughing—not her hot forehead—that makes me think something is wrong.

I drop to my knees. Now I notice that her skin looks waxy and that she's breathing heavily. "Stop playing, Esther!" I don't even realize I'm shouting. "Open your eyes!"

Esther doesn't open her eyes.

"Mom! Dad!" I shout.

How can Esther, who is so fit, be sick?

Mom and Dad come running. So does Isaac. He crouches down next to me and feels Esther's forehead the way I did. He also feels the side of her neck. "She has a high fever, and her glands are swollen," he says. "*Vee* must call the doctor. Let's bring her inside. Rosetta, can you prepare some cold compresses?"

"Where are all of you?" Annette's voice is so shrill, we can hear her from inside the building.

Dad and Isaac carry Esther inside. I run ahead so I can prepare the compresses. I'm glad to have something to do.

When I reach the kitchen, I nearly crash into Annette. "What on earth have you been carrying on about? If you don't behave yourself, Rosetta, Mom and Dad will cancel our picnic!"

Chapter 8

Annette is getting too grown-up to be Dr. Gordon's patient. She said so to Mom, and Mom agreed to see whether her and Dad's doctor would take Annette for a patient, but Mom hasn't done it yet. I think that she and Dad would like to keep us little girls forever.

I may only be twelve, but I'm growing up too. This last year my body started sprouting hair in the most embarrassing places. Soon I'll also be too old to go to Dr. Gordon.

Dr. Gordon is a pediatrician. His office is in the basement of his home on Roslyn Avenue, just a few streets over from Argyle. It's always full of squawking babies wriggling in their moms' laps, as if they wished they could switch doctors too.

Mostly, we see Dr. Gordon at his office, but if there's an emergency, he makes a house call. He charges three dollars extra for that, and he arrives, as he does this afternoon, looking grim, his black leather doctor's bag tucked under his arm.

Mom and Dad shoo the rest of us away and bring Dr. Gordon upstairs to the little room that is Esther's.

Esther's door clicks shut. The rest of us mill around downstairs for a bit. Then Annette sighs dramatically and rushes up the staircase, taking two steps at a time. We all follow, even Isaac and Anne-Marie.

Annette gestures that we must keep quiet. I try pressing my ear against the door, but I can't hear a thing—only my heart thumping in my chest and the drip drop from the leaky faucet in the bathroom down the hall.

It feels like forever before the door opens. Dr. Gordon seems surprised to see us waiting there, but then he smiles, showing his neat white teeth, and I know for certain Esther is not going to die. "It's only the flu," he tells us. "Nothing to worry about. Though the rest of you would do well to keep away from the patient for a few days."

Dr. Gordon puts his hand on Isaac's shoulder. "You must be Isaac. Those cold compresses were a good idea, young man. And I understand you were the one to notice Esther's glands were swollen. Most astute."

The corners of Isaac's lips turn up a little, and I wonder whether he is about to smile. I suddenly realize that in the two weeks Isaac has been with us I have never seen him smile.

"Might I be right in supposing you have an interest in medicine?" Dr. Gordon asks Isaac.

Isaac drops his eyes to the ground, and when he speaks, it's as if he's talking to the floor. "*Vhy*, yes, I do. *Vee* had a family friend in Düsseldorf—a physician whom I admired greatly. Sometimes, he let me come along when he visited patients." Isaac pauses to give himself a rest from so much speaking. "It's my dream to be a physician one day too."

Mom claps her hands. "Oh, Isaac," she says, "how grand!"

Dr. Gordon adjusts his glasses. "It's a noble profession, if I say so myself. May I ask whether you are planning to apply to McGill University?"

"*Zat* is my plan."

"A fine plan, I'd call it. Though if I might offer a word of advice, I'd say it's generally wise to have a contingency plan. Just in case."

"Why would Isaac need a contingency plan?" I ask.

Dr. Gordon tucks his doctor's bag under his arm.

It's not hard to tell he wants to go, that he has other patients to see before he can return home to his wife. "McGill has a very strict admissions policy. They have a quota on the number of your people they allow in."

"Our people?" This time it's Annette who asks the question.

"Yes, your people. Jews, I mean. I'm assuming Isaac is Jewish, considering he's come to live with you. And let's be frank, Isaac, you're not just a Jew. From what your . . . um . . . your father . . . has told me, you've spent some time in an internment camp here in Quebec. That will be, I'm afraid, two strikes against you. Of course, I wish you luck. And if you do apply, I'd be happy to put in a word for you."

I've never heard the word *quota* before. "A *quota*," I say, "sounds like the name of a bird."

Dad shakes his head. "I wish it were, Ronald," he says, "I wish it were."

***

I don't believe in secrets. That isn't exactly true. What I mean is I don't believe people should keep secrets from *me*. I also believe I have a talent for uncovering people's secrets. How come not Isaac's?

It's not that Isaac doesn't say anything. But mostly he asks questions ("has Esther ever run a high fever like this before?") or makes observations ("Rosetta, you have the curliest hair I have ever *zeen*"). But I have noticed he hardly ever reveals anything about himself. I've decided he really must be marked by the war and by his stay in the internment camp. I've also decided I'm going to be the one to worm his secrets out of him. Only it's much harder than I expected.

I am at the dining room table, writing to Granny . . .

Dearest Granny,

How are things in England? I hope you are safe and well. I think of you often and try to behave in a way that would make you proud of me. Sometimes, of course, that is difficult. For instance, an awful thing happened when I was competing in the first round of this year's public speaking competition. A pair of Mom's underpants somehow managed to get trapped inside my tunic, and everyone laughed at me. Though I'd have liked to run off the stage right then and there, I persevered, though I cannot say I did a very good job of it. I hope you will not be too disappointed in me.

Esther has the flu, and we are all supposed to keep our distance for a few days.

Isaac is well. Dad is glad to have a son who shares his interest in stamp collecting. Though, of course, Isaac isn't really his son, any more than he is really our brother, or your grandson. Did you know Isaac wants to become a doctor? I have noticed that he hardly ever smiles. He also doesn't say much about himself. Mom says I mustn't pry, but sometimes I can't help mys . . .

I am in mid-sentence when Isaac gets home.

"How is Esther?" he calls out. He's come in on his shoes, but then he catches himself, walks back to the hallway, and unlaces them.

I put down my pen and go to meet him at the front door. "She's a little better. Her fever's down, and she had toast and tea at lunch. Were you at McGill?" The campus is in the middle of downtown, so Isaac could easily have walked there or taken the trolleybus.

"No," Isaac says. I have noticed that people who keep secrets keep their answers short.

"Well, where were you, then?"

Instead of answering, Isaac asks *me* a question.

It's another trick secret keepers use. "Have you been doing homework, or are you writing a letter?"

"Are you trying to change topics?"

Isaac laughs. He has a raspy laugh, as if he hasn't used it much lately. But when he laughs, his face softens. For a moment, I am struck by how strange it is to have Isaac in our household.

Isaac still hasn't said where he's been. Now I feel his dark eyes on me. "If you don't mind my asking, Rosetta"—he pauses for a moment—"Why do you think you are such a curious person?"

"I . . . I don't know. Maybe because I love stories. Stories in books, stories I overhear." Have I said too much? I don't want Isaac to guess I sometimes listen in on conversations from underneath Granny's table. "Sometimes the stories people tell are as interesting as the ones in books . . . So, where did you say you were this afternoon?"

"I didn't say anything about it."

"Fine," I say, turning my back on Isaac, "besides, I don't really want to know."

Now Isaac laughs even harder. "You're not a very good liar," he says, following me into the dining room and taking the seat across from mine.

Anne-Marie peeps into the room. She has a

half-peeled potato in one hand. "Isaac, I'm making *purée de pomme de terre*—mashed potatoes. Unless you want baked potatoes instead." Though Anne-Marie might not have wanted Isaac to join our household, I think she is growing fond of him. Maybe he reminds her of Jean-Claude. Or maybe she just likes having someone around who so enjoys her cooking.

"I do like your mashed potatoes, Anne-Marie," Isaac tells her.

"Mashed potatoes all around, then." Anne-Marie heads back to the kitchen.

"So where *did* you spend the afternoon?" I ask Isaac.

This time, Isaac surprises me by answering. "I was at the Canadian Jewish Congress. Making inquiries."

"Making inquiries?" I say, hoping to get a little more information out of Isaac.

Not that he's making things easy for me. Someone without my talent for uncovering secrets would have given up by now.

When Isaac does not answer, I try a more roundabout question. "Did you see Mrs. Etkowitz from synagogue? She works there. I'm friends with her daughter Bertha."

"No I didn't."

The roundabout method does not seem to be working. "What kind of inquiries?"

Isaac has begun inspecting one of his fingernails.

"Inquiries about relatives," Isaac says. "I am trying to find out what happened to my aunt. My father's sister."

I don't need to ask Isaac whether the woman in the photograph by his bed is his aunt. Because now I know that's exactly who she is.

Chapter 9

We're usually all sound asleep by ten at night. Dad says the hours of sleep we get before midnight count for double. I don't know if it's true, or if it's Dad's way of making us go to sleep so he and Mom can have some time to themselves.

It's nearly two when I get up to use the bathroom, and though I figure that I'll be the only one up, I'm not.

There's a stripe of yellow light coming from under the door to Mom and Dad's room. Mom must have put on the light by her bedside so she can work on a poem. The thought that she is creating something beautiful at this hour makes me happy. I wish I could tell her so, but then I'd wake up Dad. The one thing that makes Dad grumpy is when his sleep is interrupted. Which is why he wears a cotton eye mask to bed—in case Mom gets a poetic urge.

I wonder what Mom's latest poem is about. I'll ask her in the morning, though she sometimes doesn't like to discuss her poems until they're done.

On my way back from the bathroom, I pause outside Esther's room. Even from the hallway, I hear her labored breathing. It sounds as if there's something stuck inside her chest, and I suddenly remember how, last fall, the chimney sweeper found a dead squirrel inside our chimney. We knew it was a squirrel from its charred skeleton. We thought it was the scariest thing we'd ever seen, but Mom wrote a poem about that squirrel. "Poems," she said afterward, "don't always have to be about beautiful things. Sometimes terrible things make better subjects. More interesting subjects."

"Esther? Are you okay in there?" I whisper from the hallway. Maybe I can get her something. Or I could rearrange her pillows so she'll breathe more easily.

"Is that you, Rosetta?" Esther's voice sounds more throaty than a bullfrog's.

I open the door and walk over to Esther's bed. Her eyes shine in the dark like watery stars. When I lean over to fluff her pillows, I notice the top pillow-case is damp. The fever must be back. "Esther, can I bring you a glass of water?"

"Yes, please," she gulps when she speaks. "If it isn't too much trouble."

I squeeze her hand. Even her fingers feel warm. "Of course, it isn't too much trouble. I'll be right back."

Because the floors creak, I take the smallest steps I can when I go down to the kitchen and back up again with Esther's water.

"Oh, that's good," she says, when I help her to sit up and take a few sips. "But you mustn't stay, Rosetta. I might still be contagious."

I turn the top pillow over so Esther can rest her face on the dry side. "A fever's always worse at night," I tell her as I brush the hair away from her forehead. When I say so, I realize I'm not only trying to comfort Esther but myself too.

★ ★ ★

Another door clicks open as I shut Esther's door behind me. Who else is up at this hour? This house is beginning to feel like Windsor Station at rush hour!

A little moonlight has slipped in through the skylight over the staircase. The light lands on the blue plaid design of a man's slipper. Those slippers came in the package Granny sent after she learned Isaac had come to live with us.

"Isaac?" I whisper into the darkness. "Is that you?"

"Yes," he whispers back.

At first, I think he needs to use the bathroom too, and so I make room for him to pass me in the hallway. Only he doesn't step forward as I expect him to.

"Is something wrong?"

"I couldn't sleep," he says. "Were you with Esther? How is she?"

"I think the fever's back. I brought her some water. She's resting." I can't think of what else to say. It feels strange to make conversation in the dark. "Have you tried counting sheep?" I finally blurt out.

"Rosetta," Isaac says, and there's something in his voice I haven't heard before—something a little lost—"would you mind sitting up with me awhile? Not for long . . ."

Because I'm not feeling so tired anymore, but mostly because of the something in Isaac's voice, I say yes.

I follow Isaac back downstairs and into the kitchen. I put on the kettle and take two cups from the cabinet. Isaac is sitting at the breakfast nook, resting his chin on his hands. The nook only seats four, so we don't use it much. A lone bird chirps outside. Perhaps he can't sleep either.

"I had a bad dream," Isaac says when I hand him a steaming cup of tea.

I know asking Isaac questions does not work. This time, I'll wait him out. I blow over my teacup. Little ripples form on the liquid surface.

"I dreamt about my aunt."

I nod, but I don't say a thing. I'm afraid if I do, I'll break the spell and Isaac will stop talking.

"Tante Dora raised me. She has no children of her own, so she was glad to take me in." Isaac stops to take a sip of tea. "After my father's death, Tante Dora took over his insurance business. But when the Nazis came to power, they wouldn't let her keep the business. She must have spent everything she had to get me on a Kindertransport—one of the trains that brought German Jewish children to England. In my dream, there was a thick gray fog and I heard Tante Dora calling for me over and over again. But I couldn't see her."

"What about your mother?" There, I've asked a question after all. I couldn't help it.

There is something about the dark that seems to make it easier for Isaac to talk to me. I know this because he answers my question.

"My mother's dead." Isaac says without any feeling. My own heart feels as if it's stopped. Both of Isaac's parents are dead. Gone forever. If that happened to me—if both my parents died—well, then, I'd die too. I want to tell Isaac how sorry I am and also to ask how his mother died, but Isaac is speaking again. "My mother was Christian. To her, because I'm half Jewish, I was a problem."

I cover my mouth. What is Isaac saying? It doesn't make any sense at all!

"In my mind," he continues, "my mother died the day she gave me up. It's Tante Dora I can't stop thinking about."

"The last time I saw her was at the train station in Düsseldorf. When I pressed my face against the glass, I saw her waving her blue handkerchief. She knew I was afraid to go to a new country, and I understand now that she must have been afraid for me, too, though she never let on. 'You'll meet the queen of England,' she told me before I left—and

71

you know what? I really thought I would."

"Tante Dora sacrificed everything she had to get me on that Kindertransport. She had to post a guarantee of fifty British pounds. An enormous sum. On the train, we older children did our best to look after the little ones. Some were younger even than Esther. We sang German *lieder*—songs—to them. But even when I was singing or bouncing one of the little ones on my lap, I was thinking of Tante Dora. Wondering if I'd ever see her again."

"During my first six months in Britain, I got letters from her—through the Red Cross. Each letter could not be more than twenty-five words long. The same rule applied to our answers. Tante Dora said that life was getting more and more difficult and that she was glad I got away in time. But then, suddenly, the letters stopped. The Red Cross had no information."

"The people at the Canadian Jewish Congress have agreed to look into Tante Dora's case. They say she's no longer living in her apartment, but they have no idea what's become of her."

Isaac rubs his eyes. I don't know if it's because they're sandy from sleep or if he is crying.

"Oh, Isaac," I tell him, "I wish there was something I could do to help you in your search."

To my surprise, Isaac laughs when I say this. "You're just a girl," he says. "There's nothing you can do to help."

That bothers me. Just because I'm a girl doesn't mean I cannot find some way to help. "That isn't true," I say.

Isaac isn't listening. "Nothing," he says again. He shakes his head as if he wishes he could make his dark thoughts go away.

Isaac's voice sounds as if it's coming from through a tunnel. For a moment, I wonder whether I am dreaming all of this—this conversation with Isaac over tea at two in the morning in our breakfast nook. But then I touch my elbow, and when I feel skin I know it's not a dream.

Chapter 10

When I step into the rowboat, my elbow brushes against Broderick's. But I don't think he's noticed because he says, "You two girls in the back!"

Glynnis and I scramble to the stern.

Broderick is still barking instructions. "Isaac, you sit up front. I'll row."

Isaac and I have been invited to spend the day at the Benbows' country home in Shawbridge, a village in the foothills of the Laurentian Mountains, north of Montreal. The Benbows wanted to take advantage of the warm weekend. Though it's nearly the end of September, Mrs. Benbow thought we might get in one last swim.

The Benbows' home, which feels more like a castle to me, is on the edge of a lake. The water is so clear we can see the sandy bottom and schools of minnows swimming this way and that, as if they are in a big hurry to get someplace.

Glynnis and I have been trying to encourage a friendship between Broderick and Isaac. Inviting Isaac to Shawbridge was Glynnis's idea. "Broderick wasn't too thrilled," Glynnis told me, "but I explained how it would be a kind gesture to reach out to a—" (Glynnis dropped her voice) "a refugee." I left out that part when I told Isaac about the invitation.

Though Broderick Benbow treats me as if I'm invisible, he is not invisible to me. Tall with wavy blond hair that he's always pushing away from his eyes, Broderick is the handsomest boy I've ever seen.

"That's right, Isaac. Sit right in the middle. And don't forget your life jacket. I expect you're not much of a swimmer."

Isaac doesn't bother answering, but when he puts on his life jacket, he gives me a tight smile.

Although he is handsome, Broderick is even bossier than Annette. He supervises while Glynnis and I fasten our life jackets. "No, no, do it this way," he says adjusting the top clip on Glynnis's jacket.

"It's because he's applied to the Faculty of

Medicine at McGill," Glynnis whispers to me. "He's going all doctor-y on us. He made a huge fuss the other day when Mother nicked herself with a paring knife. You'd have thought he was performing open-heart surgery."

"Did you hear that, Isaac?" I say to Isaac, who is looking out toward the other side of the lake where a mother mallard is fussing over her ducklings. "Broderick has applied to the Faculty of Medicine too."

Broderick rows so hard he makes waves in the lake water. "I think I stand an excellent chance of being accepted," he says. "Not just because I have the grades, but also because I go to Selwyn House"— Broderick's chest puffs up when he says this— "a school the admissions committee looks favorably upon. Of course it doesn't hurt that our father is on the admissions committee."

"He *ees*?" Isaac seems to have forgotten the duck family.

"Yes, he *ees*," Broderick says, imitating Isaac's accent. Isaac's face reddens. For a moment, Broderick releases his hands from the oars, letting them rest on the boat. "I'm only teasing, my good man," he tells Isaac. "You can take a joke, can't you?"

Isaac nods in response. Maybe he's afraid that if he says something more, Broderick will do another imitation.

Broderick begins to paddle again. "Glynnis told me you've applied too," he says to Isaac as he rows us out to the middle of the lake. "I wish you luck." Broderick clears his throat. "You're going to need it."

Maybe I should have stood up for Isaac. It was mean of Broderick to mimic Isaac's accent, even if Broderick said he was teasing. It's not as if he's Esther's age, so really, he should know better. But I don't say anything. The day is too sunny. The water is too clear for stirring up trouble.

"I do hope you're not planning to give up on your public speaking career," Glynnis is saying. I feel my ears get hot. I hope Broderick hasn't heard the story of Mom's underpants.

"I'm just taking a break," I tell Glynnis. I don't want Broderick to think I'm a quitter.

Glynnis reaches over and adjusts my sun hat so it covers more of my face. "What's the point of a sun hat if you don't have it on right?" she says. Her tone is harsh, but I know Glynnis is looking out for me. She doesn't want me getting a sunburn.

Broderick, too, often speaks in a harsh tone. But maybe his harshness is only on the outside, like Glynnis's. Underneath, he must be a caring person too. Why else would he want to become a doctor?

★ ★ ★

Glynnis has spotted a giant tortoise sunning himself on a nearby rock that is jutting out of the water. "Row us over to see him!" she tells Broderick. "He's so big he must be a thousand years old."

In about five strokes, Broderick has us there, and Glynnis is peering at the tortoise. When she gives his shell a poke, the tortoise's head disappears. "Not a very friendly creature, are you?" Glynnis tells him.

"He'd probably prefer not to be *dees-turbed*," says Isaac. "That's how I'd feel if I were him."

I can't help giggling when Isaac says that. "It's true," I tell the others. "Isaac doesn't like being poked or prodded, especially with questions."

"Is that so?" says Broderick, squinting as he looks at Isaac. "I hope it isn't because you've got something to hide."

Isaac shrugs. "It's getting warm," he says,

stretching out his arms. "Am I the only one who feels like going for a swim?"

Broderick says he'd prefer to get some more rowing in, but Glynnis and I feel like a dip too. The water's surface is warm, but underneath, it's much colder—so cold I get goose bumps on my legs. Splashing helps warm us up. Two dragonflies with gossamer wings land on the water, do an elegant dance, and then fly off. The tortoise's head has popped out again from inside his shell, and now he's the one watching us. His eyes look very old.

Glynnis is showing Isaac how well she can tread water. It turns out that though Isaac is a strong swimmer, he's not much good at treading. "I'm more used to moving than to *stending* still," he sputters.

"Come back to get us, Broderick!" Glynnis's voice echoes across the lake.

"My legs are freezing up!" Glynnis adds, when after a few minutes, Broderick still has not turned the rowboat back in our direction.

"Your lips are turning purple," I tell Glynnis, and when I say so, I can feel my teeth chatter.

Broderick takes his sweet time coming to get us. "Not very doctor-y of him," I whisper to Glynnis when we're climbing back into the rowboat. "We could have caught pneumonia out there."

Glynnis and I are huddled so close in the stern that our thighs touch. I feel sorry for Isaac, who is sitting all alone in the bow.

"So I don't imagine you got much schooling in that internment camp," Broderick says to Isaac. Though I'm glad Broderick is making an effort to talk to Isaac, again there is something unkind in Broderick's tone. It's clear Broderick shares Glynnis's and Anne-Marie's low opinion of internment camps and the people in them.

"You're right about *zat*," Isaac says, without turning round to look at Broderick. "We got no schooling at all in the internment camp. Fortunately, I got a rather good education at the *gymnasium* in Düsseldorf. We did Latin and Greek—and all the sciences. Of course, my studies were interrupted when . . ." Isaac lets his voice trail off.

"When what?" Broderick asks impatiently.

"When the National Socialists barred those of us with Jewish blood from attending school." Isaac's thin back trembles at the memory, and I hope that, now, Broderick will know enough to drop the conversation.

But Broderick does not seem to notice Isaac's

reaction. "And now we have to deal with all you Jews wanting to get into Canada and trying to take our places at medical school."

Now Isaac whips round to face Broderick. Isaac's dark eyes have a wild look. "*All you Jews?*" This time, it's Isaac who is mimicking Broderick. "Believe me, Broderick, there are far more Jews who are dead in Europe—killed by the Nazis—than will ever turn up in your country."

Glynnis is clutching my elbow.

Broderick throws back his shoulders. "Some people say you Jews are like pigs coming to the trough, and the trough is this fine country."

Isaac stands up, causing the rowboat to lurch to one side.

Glynnis screams.

I know I should stand up for Isaac and say what I am thinking: that Broderick is behaving in a horrible way and that he is insulting me, too, because I am even more Jewish than Isaac. But I don't want to make a fuss, especially not today, when we are the Benbows' guests in Shawbridge.

"Isaac," I say, "sit down this instant!"

From the look on Isaac's face, I'm afraid he is about to throttle Broderick.

"Broderick meant nothing by it, Isaac," Glynnis adds. "Did you, Broderick?"

Isaac returns to his seat, but I can hear him breathing heavily.

"That's right. I meant nothing by it." Broderick sounds sorry. Because of how we're sitting, I'm the only one who can see the smirk on his handsome face.

Chapter 11

It's Saturday morning, and we're on our way to shul. Mom and Dad are a little ways ahead of Annette, Isaac, and me. Esther, who is still on bed rest—and not too happy about it—is home with Anne-Marie.

Isaac has promised to walk with both of us. Since it takes thirty minutes to walk from Argyle Avenue to shul, Annette and I will each get fifteen minutes with him. Right now, it's Annette's turn. She is wearing black patent leather heels with crisscross ankle straps. Every few steps, one or the other of Annette's ankles caves in and she looks down crossly, as if the shoes are misbehaving. Why didn't she practice walking in them first?

I'm a few steps behind Annette and Isaac.

We've just passed the Church of St. Leon. There are nearly as many church steeples as chimneys in

Westmount, but St. Leon is the only one that's for Catholics. Up ahead, I can see that Mom and Dad are nearly at Atwater Avenue. Because it's such a busy intersection, they'll wait for us. Dad must've said something silly because Mom just tweaked his nose.

Atwater is where Westmount ends and downtown Montreal begins. The streets and sidewalks are more crowded, and the skyscrapers that loomed in the distance before are coming closer. We're not far now from the tallest of them all—the Sun Life Building on Dorchester Square.

Though it's Shabbos, our day of rest, Montreal is wide awake. Cars honk at one another impatiently, and I hear piano music coming from an upstairs apartment. A boy at the corner of Atwater and Sherbrooke is flogging copies of the *Gazette*. "We have home delivery," Dad says and wishes the boy a good day. Across the street, a French-speaking boy asks passersby if they want to buy a copy of *Le Journal de Montréal*.

"It's my turn now to walk with Isaac," I say when we're all at the corner.

"Fine!" Annette says, rolling her eyes to tell me I am being difficult.

"It's only fair!" I tell her. "He's my brother too!"

Isaac and Dad are both wearing yarmulkes, the skullcaps Jewish men wear for prayer. Isaac has borrowed one of Dad's spare yarmulkes.

"Did you have your own yarmulke in Düsseldorf?" I ask Isaac, and then I bite my lip. I know we're not supposed to say anything that could remind Isaac of his past. I just can't seem to help it.

Isaac looks down at the sidewalk when he answers. "I didn't go to synagogue very often. Only sometimes, and then it was mostly to please my *tante*."

As usual, Isaac hasn't answered my question. "Does that mean you *didn't* have a yarmulke?"

Isaac sighs, and now he turns to look at me. "Yes, Rosetta, I had a yarmulke. Of course, I would never have worn it on the street—not after 1938. My yarmulke was pale blue; my *tante* crocheted it for me. But it was lost—like *every-ting else*." I know Isaac doesn't mean lost as in misplaced, the way Mom is always losing her magnifying loupe.

"So," I say to Isaac, "coming to synagogue today. It's something you're doing for Dad? The way you went to synagogue in Düsseldorf to make your aunt happy?"

"I suppose so."

"Don't you believe in God?" I ask Isaac.

"Do you, Rosetta?" There! He's gone and turned the question round again. "*Do* you?"

"Why, of course I do," I say, only when I hear my own voice, it doesn't sound like I'm so sure of it. Why *do* I go to synagogue? I never had much choice about it. Going to synagogue is as much a part of my life as . . . as brushing my teeth . . . or having oatmeal for breakfast. They're all things I do without stopping to ask why I do them. Besides, how can I expect God to listen to my prayers if I don't go to synagogue and follow the rules of my religion?

I think Isaac can tell I'm confused because when he speaks, his tone is gentler. "It's not," he says, "that I *don't* believe. I *can't* believe."

Can't believe?" I turn to look at him. It bothers me that he sounds so sure of what he's said. Especially since it doesn't make any sense! Anyone *can* believe. "What do you mean?"

"I just can't believe," he says as if the matter is settled. "Not after *every-ting* I've seen. There is no God." Isaac watches my face when he says this, the way I watched Glynnis's when I told her there was no Santa Claus, as if he's worried he might be spoiling things for me. "No God could allow the sorts of *tings* I saw in Germany. No God could allow a man like Hitler to exist. No God could allow humans to turn on each other . . . like . . . like animals. But you couldn't possibly understand any of this. You . . . you . . ." and now there is something accusing in Isaac's voice, "you have *every-ting*."

Up ahead, I see Mom and Dad, arm in arm; from behind, I hear the clop of Annette's black shoes. I think of Esther, lying on the couch at home, probably trying to do sit-ups when Anne-Marie isn't watching . . . and I decide Isaac is right. I do have everything.

I just never realized it before.

***

Mom and Dad want a turn to walk with Isaac too. Again, I feel a stab of jealousy. And to make things even worse, now I'm stuck with Annette, who will want to talk about pencil skirts or military-style buttons on women's jackets. But that isn't what Annette has on her mind.

"What were you two yakking about?" Annette sounds annoyed, as if I'm a fly she wants to swat. "You and Isaac looked so . . . so serious."

"Nothing in particular," I tell her.

And because Annette is nothing like me, she doesn't ask again.

The traffic, both on the street and sidewalk, is even heavier now. We're nearly at the giant church at the corner of Mackay and Sherbrooke Streets, and soon we'll be at shul.

Two young men, sailors, are walking toward us. I see one nudge the other when he spots first Dad's, and then Isaac's, yarmulke. "Jews," the first one says under his breath. "And here comes a pretty one and her little sister."

They tip their sailors' hats when they pass us. Annette gives them each a smile.

"I admire a man in uniform," Annette says when the sailors are not quite out of earshot. One of them turns around and waves at us.

"Annette! How can you be so forward?" I ask her, though I can't help giggling a little.

"Look!" Annette says when we are within view of the shul. "Across the street. Sarah Fineberg is wearing so much rouge you'd think she was a circus clown."

On the sidewalk in front of the shul, members of our congregation are greeting one another. The men shake hands; the women kiss one another's cheeks. Bertha must already be inside, saving me a seat.

Dad is introducing Isaac to Mr. Etkowitz, Bertha's father. Mr. Etkowitz is also our kosher butcher, though with the new rationing system, we are all having to manage with less meat than usual.

"So you've finally got yourself a son," Mr. Etkowitz is saying. "Now your family is complete."

"A family doesn't need a son to be complete," I tell Mr. Etkowitz.

Mr. Etkowitz seems surprised that I've spoken to him. He pats my shoulder. "I'm only saying that there's something special about a man's relationship with his son." I think of how Dad always calls us by boys' names. It's just a joke—or isn't it?

"There is certainly something special about a man's relationship with his daughters," Isaac adds.

"Indeed," Mr. Etkowitz says, turning back to face Isaac. "Once they fatten you up with some of my fine *fleisch*, young man, you'll look almost as Canadian as the rest of us." I notice Isaac eyeing Mr. Etkowitz's belly, which sticks out like a mountaintop over his trousers.

"You did a good thing," Mr. Etkowitz tells Dad, "by taking in this young man. I take it you also had a visit from that fellow Schwartzberg."

"As a matter of fact, we did. A courageous man if I ever met one," Dad says.

"I hear he'll be back in town in a week or two," Mr. Etkowitz tells Dad. "He stays in a boarding-house near my shop."

Isaac and I are standing side by side now. "I was thinking about our conversation," he says, "and there's something else I want to say . . . about coming to synagogue."

"Well, then, go ahead and say it!"

Isaac looks very serious, and I am sorry for teasing him. "I may not believe in God" he says. "But what I saw in Germany and later in the internment camp"—he closes his eyes for a moment as if he is picturing it all again—"made me realize that even if my mother was a gentile, I consider myself a Jew and that if ever Jews are criticized or attacked, I'll be the first to stand up to defend them and myself."

I get a heavy feeling in my belly because I am remembering our visit to Shawbridge. I didn't stand up when Broderick made that comment about Jews and swine.

"I'm sorry about Shawbridge," I say, though it could be too late for an apology.

Isaac shrugs. "That Broderick," he says, "is a dummkopf."

"A dummkopf?"

Isaac pauses for a minute, and I can almost see his mind working, sorting through the dictionary he must keep in his brain. "Blockhead!" he says, grinning because he's found the right word.

* * *

Bertha shushes me when I try whispering to her during the rabbi's sermon. "Not now," she says, mouthing the words—and I can't help thinking Glynnis is right: Bertha is not much fun.

After services, there is tea and Bertha suspends her no-talking rule. "Wasn't the rabbi's sermon inspiring?" she asks me.

I don't admit I was daydreaming. "Very," I tell her instead.

"How are things going with Isaac?" she asks. "Having an extra person in the house must be difficult sometimes. Does he leave his wet towel on the bathroom floor the way Solomon does?" Solomon is Bertha's little brother. He is Esther's age.

"Sometimes. But all in all, I'd say things are

going well. I like having a brother." I suddenly picture Dad and Isaac sharing the loupe as they examine stamps together. "Mostly."

Bertha laughs. "A big brother might be better than a little one," she says wistfully.

I turn around to make sure that my parents—and Isaac—are nowhere nearby. "Isaac has been making inquiries about a relative in Düsseldorf. So far, he hasn't had any luck. Do you think your mother might be able to help? I know she works for Mr. Bronfman at the Canadian Jewish Congress."

"I can ask," Bertha says. "What about Mr. Schwartzberg? Have you thought about speaking to him?"

"I would if I knew where to find him."

When Bertha smiles, she reminds me a little of the cat in the *Alice* book. "I may be able to help you with that."

Chapter 12

"Girls!" Miss Vipond's forehead furrows the way it does when she's upset.

My face heats up. Has Miss Vipond spotted the tiny folded up piece of paper on my desk—the note Glynnis just passed me?

"Rosetta," Miss Vipond says, "Can you tell us which Latin verb we are currently conjugating?"

"Uhh . . ." I am stalling for time.

"Glynnis? Perhaps you know the answer."

"I'm afraid I don't."

I watch as Miss Vipond's eyes land on Glynnis's note. I'm nearly sure we're about to get a detention. "The verb is *statum*, 'to stand up.' We'll conjugate it together."

I have to wait to read Glynnis's note until two verbs later, when Miss Vipond is calling on students at the back of the classroom. I use the tip of my pencil to unfold the note, and then I leave it lying on my desk so I'll be able to read it from a safe distance. Luckily, I have not inherited Mom's bad eyes.

I can't believe I nearly forgot to tell you the wonderful news! Broderick has had an early acceptance from McGill Medical School. Dr. Benbow!!! I'm so pleased for him, though now, he'll be even more conceited (if such a thing is possible)! You must promise not to say a thing since the news is not yet official. Has Isaac had word?
    G

I don't risk writing back to Glynnis. Not with Miss Vipond on high alert! I'm glad for Broderick, of course. I can already picture him with a gleaming stethoscope hanging from around his neck. But even in my imagination, Broderick is not so handsome anymore. He's sneering the way he did that afternoon in Shawbridge, when he made that awful comment about Jews and pigs.

As for Isaac, I'm nearly sure he has not heard from McGill yet. He'd tell us if there was news—or would he? Isaac is more full of secrets than anyone I know.

The postman is just leaving when I get home. Mom is sorting through the mail; Isaac hovers nearby. "Nothing here," Mom says, "except a bill for school taxes and a flyer from Simpson's. I'm sorry, Isaac."

I'm glad I've promised to keep the news of Broderick's early acceptance to McGill a secret.

"I think I'll go upstairs . . . to work on my stamps," Isaac announces. For a moment, I think about asking if he'd like my help, but then I decide not to. Something about the look in Isaac's eyes tells me that he wants to be left alone, at least for now.

Mom must notice too. "My heart breaks for that young man," she says once Isaac's door clicks shut. "Sometimes I think not knowing is the hardest thing. Just look at Anne-Marie. She's suffering, too."

That is when I decide to take matters into my own hands. Tomorrow I will take some action. Though there is nothing I can do to find out whether Anne-Marie's brother is all right or to speed up Isaac's answer from McGill, there may be something I can do to learn about what's happened to his Tante Dora.

Bertha told me Mr. Schwartzberg's rooming house is in the east end of the city, at the corner of St. Viateur and Park Avenue. She knew because her father asked her and Solomon to deliver a few slices of brisket to Mr. Schwartzberg when he first arrived in Montreal. She even remembered the street address. "I'm afraid I can't remember the room number," she told me, "but that isn't so important. Besides, he might be staying in another room this time."

I have to take two trolleybuses and then do quite a lot of walking to get there. I pass kids playing ball at Fletcher's Field. When I reach St. Viateur, I smell the bagel store before I see it. Nothing smells as delicious as fresh bagels. And there's Mr. Etkowitz's butcher shop.

Mr. Schwartzberg's building is just around the corner. It's a small gray stone walk-up. I'm wondering how I'm going to find Mr. Schwartzberg's room when he walks into the small lobby. The air stinks of cooked cabbage.

"Mr. Schwartzberg!" I call out.

His back stiffens when he hears his name and again, I'm reminded of a fox. His dark eyes dart quickly around the lobby before they settle on me.

"Do I know you?" Mr. Schwartzberg is still wearing too-big trousers, but his face is not as thin as it was before.

"I'm Rosetta Wolfson. You visited our house . . . on Argyle Avenue."

"Oh, yes," he says, "I remember. That was you hiding underneath the table, wasn't it?"

I feel myself blush. But there doesn't seem to be much point in lying. "Yes," I tell him, meeting his gaze, "that was me."

Mr. Schwartzberg doesn't seem to think any less of me. "Well, then, Rosetta, *vut* brings you here?"

"I wanted to ask you for some help. It's for a friend."

Mr. Schwartzberg takes a packet of cigarettes from his pocket. "I was just going to the luncheonette. We can talk there," he says, fishing out a cigarette and lighting it. His fingertips are stained yellow from nicotine.

The luncheonette is across Park Avenue. It has a counter with tall chrome swivel chairs. The waitress brings Mr. Schwartzberg a mug of mucky-looking coffee before he even has a chance to order. There is a pencil tucked behind her ear. I order an orange soda.

A woman with hair dyed so black it looks like a helmet is getting up from another swivel chair. "I don't know how you drink that stuff black," she says, eyeing Mr. Schwartzberg's coffee. "The damned sugar rations are killing me."

Mr. Schwartzberg nods politely, but he doesn't say anything.

"*Bonne journée*," the waitress says to helmet head. "Have yourself a good day now. Sorry about the sugar. But they say they need it for the war—to make explosives."

"I hear they're going to ration coffee and tea next," helmet head grumbles. "And then what'll become of us?"

The bell on the luncheonette door jingles when she leaves.

Mr. Schwartzberg sighs. "There are worse things in the world," he says, "than taking your coffee black."

The waitress is washing down the counter. She moves a copy of the day's *Gazette* out of the way. "So what do you make of what happened in Dieppe?" she asks Mr. Schwartzberg. She speaks with a French accent.

"It isn't good." Mr. Schwartzberg shakes his head. "Too many lives lost and, from what I can tell, not enough gained. The *Gazette* would have us believe the raid was a great triumph, but that isn't what the Ottawa paper is saying."

He makes slurping sounds when he drinks his coffee. "I heard the news," he says, looking up at me as if he's just remembered I'm sitting next to him, "*zat* your parents took in a refugee boy. Very good of *dem*. Of all of you, I should say. How is *dee* boy doing?"

"Fine," I say. Then I think about how this afternoon Isaac locked himself in his bedroom and about how he has trouble sleeping, and suddenly, I'm not so sure Isaac really is fine.

"He needs time. Like all of us," Mr. Schwartzberg says. "I understand he came on one of *dee* Kindertransports."

"It's Isaac—my new brother—I came to talk to you about," I tell Mr. Schwartzberg. It's the first time I've used the word *brother* aloud to describe Isaac, and it feels strange and nice at the same time. "Actually, it's about his Tante Dora."

Mr. Schwartzberg rests his mug on the counter and lights another cigarette. "I see," he says, between puffs, and somehow I get the feeling that Mr. Schwartzberg sees a lot.

"Isaac was very close with his Tante Dora. He lived with her in Düsseldorf, and she was very kind to him. From what he's told me, he was closer to her than he was to his own moth—"

"The tante's name is Dora? Dora Guttman?"

Mr. Schwartzberg seems to have forgotten all about his cigarette, which is turning into a thin trail of gray ash on the edge of his saucer.

"Yes," I say, "I'm quite sure. Because the aunt is the sister of Isaac's father, who died some years ago. His last name was Guttman."

"And this Dora lived in Düsseldorf? Are you quite sure of it?"

Mr. Schwartzberg's dark eyes look as if they might pop out of their sockets. He takes hold of my wrist. "Düsseldorf?" he asks again.

"Yes, Düsseldorf. Do you know anything about her? Isaac hasn't seen her since the day she brought him to the Kindertransport. At first, he got some letters from her, but then they stopped. It would ease his mind to know she is alive and well. I think he loves her more than anyone." I know I'm babbling, but something about the look in Mr. Schwartzberg's eyes makes me nervous. As if he's forgotten all about me and the luncheonette. As if he is somewhere else altogether.

"I had a cousin in Moravia," Mr. Schwarzberg says. "Lenka. We grew up together. She was on the cattle car too." Mr. Schwartzberg's Adam's apple wobbles in his throat. "Even as a small child, Lenka was always making friends, talking with strangers. She was like *zat* all her life. Even on the cattle car. Imagine making friends on a cattle car . . ."

I'm afraid his wartime experience has affected Mr. Schwartzberg's brain. Why is he telling me about his cousin Lenka? "What does any of this have to do with Dora Guttman?" I ask.

Mr. Schwartzberg shakes his head as if I've woken him from a dream. "I'm coming to *zat*," he tells me. "There were two buckets on every wagon. One with drinking water in it. The Nazis told us if we had to go, to use the other bucket. In the end, no one bothered. The stench was unimaginable."

I can't help putting my hand over my nose.

"We were standing in our own waste," Mr. Schwartzberg continues, "our hands stretched into the air to make more room for the others, and like I told you, Lenka—being Lenka—made a friend." Mr. Schwartzberg laughs, but there is something dark and hollow about the sound. "A girl from Düsseldorf. Dora Guttman. I can still see her. Dark hair, high cheekbones, dark, lonely eyes."

I think of the photograph Isaac keeps by his bed. His Tante Dora has dark hair and high cheekbones; her eyes are dark, but not lonely. Maybe she changed after she had to send Isaac away. He had been like a son to her.

"What a remarkable coincidence that you crossed paths with Isaac's Tante Dora!" I say to Mr. Schwartzberg.

Mr. Schwartzberg looks confused. "Coincidence? There's no such thing. Everything under the sun happens for a reason. I believe it was fate that I met Dora Guttman."

"Do you know what happened to her?" I ask Mr. Schwartzberg. "Could she still be alive? Is there hope? Any hope at all?" I feel as if the answer matters almost as much to me as it will to Isaac. And I also feel afraid. What if it's bad news?

Mr. Schwartzberg looks at me as if he is seeing me for the first time. "The train ahead of ours broke down. So the Nazis loaded the Jews from that other train onto the one we were on, even though there was already no room. The Nazis opened the doors and shoved them in. Several people were crushed by the mob. Including my cousin Lenka and Dora Guttman. Trampled to death. There was nothing I could do to help them. I was standing by the door—and so I did the only thing I could think to do—I ran. The Nazis shot at me, but I kept running."

I try to imagine what Mr. Schwartzberg is describing, but I can't. The senselessness of those deaths. Mr. Schwartzberg escaping a shower of bullets. Does he feel guilty that he survived but that Lenka and Dora didn't? Was there anything he could have done to help them, or would his efforts have doomed him too?

Now, for the first time in my life, I see a grown man cry. "Do you understand why it is, Rosetta," Mr. Schwartzberg asks between sobs, "that I have to tell other Jews what has happened? I do it for my parents, who were on that train too, who saw all this; for my brother; and for Lenka—and Dora." Mr. Schwartzberg's nicotine-stained fingers are trembling.

The waitress brings him another paper napkin and pats his shoulder. This must not be the first time he's wept at the luncheonette.

Chapter 13

On the trolleybus home, I remember Mom's words: "Sometimes I think not knowing is the hardest thing."

Sometimes, knowing is even harder.

I can't tell Isaac about his Tante Dora. Not now. Not only because I'm afraid to break the terrible news, but because I worry the news of Dora's death will be too much for Isaac to handle. Right now, he is living with the pain of not knowing. I'm afraid that knowing what has happened to his aunt will be even worse. At least now, he can hope that she is still alive and that one day, they will be together. I don't have the heart to take that hope away.

Only I can't decide if I am being kind or cowardly.

What would I want if I were Isaac?

How would I feel if I lost my mother? The thought is almost too painful to imagine. I'd feel as if I were like a boat that came unmoored. My mother has always been there, at the center of everything, holding our family together. I can't imagine ever having to go on without her. How has Isaac managed it? Not just without his mother . . . without anybody.

A little voice inside my head says, *I think that I would want to know.*

I silence the voice. I can't tell Isaac. I don't have the courage. I'll wait for a better time. Maybe after he has been accepted into McGill's Medical School. If he is accepted.

"Rosetta," Mom calls from the parlor when I get home. "Come say hello."

My mouth falls open when I see who is sitting on our sofa, drinking Earl Grey tea and nibbling on a tea biscuit. Miss Vipond!

"What is she doing here?" I ask. Then I realize how rude I must sound. "Uh, umm, Miss Vipond. What a surprise to see you here. At our house. I—I didn't know you drank tea or ate biscuits." Oh my, that doesn't sound much better. It's just so strange to see Miss Vipond in our house—not in front of the blackboard or standing at the back of the auditorium.

Her hair's not piled in a bun; instead, it hangs loosely over her shoulders. She looks younger and less serious than she does at school.

"Even teachers drink tea and eat biscuits," Miss Vipond says, smiling. "Your mother and I have been having a delightful chat about poetry. And about your public speaking career."

"You have?" I'm glad the two of them have been discussing poetry, less glad about the public speaking.

"Rosetta, dear," Mom says, gesturing toward the armchair across from where she and Miss Vipond are sitting, "you never told me about that unfortunate incident with my underpants." Mom shakes her head sympathetically.

I sit on the edge of the chair. In case I need to make a quick getaway. "I was too embarrassed to tell you."

"Miss Vipond is worried you might give up public speaking altogether."

"I don't want to give it up altogether. Maybe just for this year. Besides, my score wasn't high enough for me to qualify for the finals."

Miss Vipond crosses her legs at the ankles. I make a mental note to cross my legs like that from now on too. One day, I want to have a pearl choker, too, just like Miss Vipond's. "I've spoken to the principal about what happened. We've decided to let you enter the finals. Despite your score."

"Aren't you pleased, Rosetta?" Mom asks when I don't react to Miss Vipond's news.

"Uh . . . of course I'm pleased," I tell the two of them. And then, finally, I remember my manners. "Thank you, Miss Vipond, for going to all this trouble for me. And for coming here today."

Mom smiles approvingly and freshens up Miss Vipond's tea.

I smile too. But my smile feels forced. I know if I ever get up to make another speech, the students in the audience will giggle and poke one another before I even get started. They'll never forget those underpants that were dangling from the back of my tunic.

* * *

Esther is getting stronger. Soon she will be well enough to go back to kindergarten. In the meantime, we are trying to keep her entertained. Mom says Esther is not to overexert herself, so there will be no games of tag or even hide-and-seek.

"What about snakes and ladders?" Esther asks.

"Are you sure you wouldn't rather I read you a fairy tale? What about 'The Story of Goldilocks and the Three Bears?'"

Esther is not interested in Goldilocks's adventures. She wants snakes and ladders.

The snakes and ladders box is in my old room—Isaac's room. When I knock on the door, Mom calls up from downstairs, "You can go right in, dear. Isaac's gone for a walk. To clear his head."

It's the first time I've been alone in my old room since Isaac joined our family. It smells a little tangy—not like smelly feet, or armpits, even, but somehow like a boy.

Tante Dora gazes out at me from her spot by Isaac's bed. I turn away, afraid to meet her gaze. I don't want to think about her terrible end. How she was trampled by her fellow Jews.

The board games are still where we always kept them—piled on a shelf at the back of my—I should say, Isaac's—closet. I'll need to move Isaac's cardboard boxes to reach the snakes and ladders. There's the box in which Isaac stores his precious stamp collection.

"Rosetta!" Esther calls from downstairs, her voice surprisingly strong for a patient. "Why are you being such a slowpoke?"

There are two boxes with stamps. Isaac must have begun his stamp collection the day he was born. How else could he have collected so many? I push the two boxes out of the way. Behind them is Isaac's third box. This one is sealed with three thick rubber bands, and there is nothing written on it. Everything about this box—the way it has been stuffed at the very back of the closet, the rubber bands—tells me that this box is special, and that whatever is inside is secret.

Top secret.

A better person would put the boxes back and just take out the snakes and ladders. A better person would respect Isaac's privacy. A better person would hurry downstairs right now and set up the game of snakes and ladders on the table in the parlor.

But I'm just me. No worse—and definitely no better.

"Esther!" I call down, making sure to use my most serious voice. "I just remembered that I have a paragraph to write for Canadian history! The miserable thing is due tomorrow! I'm going to do it now, and we'll play snakes and ladders the minute I'm done. Okay, Esther?"

Even from here, I can hear Esther sighing.

I can also hear what Mom has to say: "Oh, Esther, I know you're disappointed, but in this house, studies come first. And we must give Rosetta credit for being such a hardworking student."

I'm too busy pulling the rubber bands off Isaac's box to feel guilty.

Chapter 14

This box is much lighter than the ones filled with stamps.

When I give it a shake, nothing rattles around inside.

And when I remove the lid, I am surprised to find nothing but tissue paper so old it's gone yellow.

I give the box another shake. Just to make sure I didn't miss whatever Isaac has been hiding.

Still nothing.

I turn the box over and dump the tissue paper on the floor. When I do, a narrow strip of orange-yellow fabric comes fluttering to the ground.

What are those dark markings on the cotton? More importantly, why has Isaac bothered to bring a strip of cotton fabric with him from across the ocean?

Even when I turn the fabric over and see what is printed on it, it still takes my brain a few moments to make sense of what I am looking at.

Printed on the orange-yellow fabric is a long row of five-pointed stars of David, the Jewish star. Inside each star, in old-fashioned black lettering is the word Jude. I don't need to speak German to understand that Jude means "Jew."

Each star is outlined with perforated lines. The kind you see in paper doll cutout books. Like paper dolls, these stars are meant to be cutout. German Jews, like Isaac, must have been forced to wear these stars on their clothing so they could be identified as Jude, or Jews. The realization makes me feel a little queasy.

For some reason, I find myself picturing Isaac's Tante Dora. In my mind, she is wearing a tattered gray coat with one of these Jewish stars sewn with large, rushed stitches over the breast pocket.

Isaac, too, would have been forced to wear a star like the ones I am looking at. What did it feel like to walk the streets of Düsseldorf wearing a Jewish star? Was Isaac wearing one when he boarded the Kindertransport? Were all the children wearing Jewish stars? Did they keep theirs too?

Which makes me wonder why Isaac brought this strip of fabric with him from Germany and why he has been hiding it at the back of my (I should say *his*) closet.

Why would Isaac want to be reminded of the terrible way the Jews were treated? If it were me, I'd have burnt those stars.

Then the answer comes to me. Isaac has hidden the stars at the back of the closet because he doesn't want to be reminded of what he endured.

But he brought the stars with him because they are proof that what happened to him and to Europe's Jews really did happen. Maybe one day, Isaac will be ready to show these stars to others.

I sniff the fabric. It smells of mothballs. I run the fabric between my fingers. It's slightly rough. I think of all the German Jews who have been or who are still forced to wear stars like these. Somewhere, at this very moment in Germany, there's a girl my age wearing a badge like the one I am touching.

I don't cry; I don't even move. Instead, I sit on the floor inside my old closet, paralyzed by sorrow.

What makes me feel even worse is that I have no one to tell.

Mom and Dad would not forgive me for snooping in Isaac's private things. Isaac would be angry. And Glynnis would not understand. A little part of me worries that maybe, even if she'd never admit it, Glynnis shares some of Broderick's prejudice against Jews. Maybe it's because of that that I don't feel as close to Glynnis as I used to.

For a moment, I wonder whether I could talk to Bertha about what I've found . . . but no . . . she'd disapprove of snooping too.

I've never felt so lonely.

I take a deep breath and tuck the strip of fabric back inside the tissue paper. Then I stuff the tissue paper back into the box.

I replace the cover and reattach the rubber bands, crossing them in a *V*, exactly as Isaac had them. Then I return the box to the back of the closet, arranging the two boxes of stamps in front of it. The only thing that's missing is the sprinkling of dust that was on top of the box when I took it out of the closet. But Isaac won't notice that.

I take another deep breath before I head downstairs to play snakes and ladders with Esther. There are moments when the sound of her laughter comforts me. But when my token lands on the snake's head and I have to move all the way down to the bottom of the snake, I start to feel overwhelmed again. It's not because of the game. It's because I'm beginning to understand that Europe's Jews are being hunted and trapped and swallowed alive by something far more evil and much uglier than a snake.

Chapter 15

Mom and Anne-Marie aren't cleaning or cooking or doing laundry. When I get home from school, they're sitting in the breakfast nook. Mom is patting Anne-Marie's hand. I know right away there's news about Jean-Claude.

"Is he alive?" I ask, and then I realize that probably wasn't the best way to ask the question. "Is he?" I ask, hoping that will sound better.

"*Oui*," Anne-Marie answers, "he's alive." When she looks up at me, I see her eyes are wet. "But he's been taken prisoner by the Nazis."

"The main thing," Mom says, her voice so bright I know it's forced, "is that he is alive and that there's hope."

"You're right," Anne-Marie says, getting up from her spot and wiping her hands on her apron.

It must be a day for news. There are also two letters from Granny. With the war going on overseas, Granny's letters are less frequent. One letter is addressed just to Isaac; the other is addressed, in Granny's spidery handwriting, to all of us. How will I ever be able to wait until Dad gets home from work, and then again until after dessert, before he reads us the letter?

I know it's possible to steam a letter open by holding it over a kettle, but first, I'd have to get my hands on the letter. Which would be difficult since Mom has set it on the mahogany table and Anne-Marie is keeping careful watch over it. Sometimes I think Anne-Marie is a mind reader.

Isaac takes the letter addressed to him up to his room.

I'm about to ask whether he'd like me to be there when he reads it, but then Mom shoots me a look. She shakes her head and mouths the words, "Let him be."

Upstairs, Isaac's door clicks shut. I hear him tear open the envelope and then—nothing. No sound at all.

My imagination is working overtime. Could Granny have learned that Isaac's Tante Dora is dead? Has Granny broken the news in her letter? In a way,

I'd be glad if she had. Then I wouldn't have to keep carrying the weight of the secret.

Keeping secrets, I'm discovering, is not one of my talents, and lately, it feels as if I've become the keeper of many secrets. I'm not supposed to tell anyone about Broderick's acceptance to McGill Medical School; I'm afraid to tell Isaac about his Tante Dora; and then there is the secret of the Jewish stars.

Esther squeals when she sees that Anne-Marie is out back, taking the sheets off the line. "Will you bounce me? Please!" she asks Mom.

"I'm not sure you're strong enough yet," Mom says.

"I am! I am! Please!"

"All right, then, we'll bounce you," Mom says. "But just a little."

I have not said anything to Anne-Marie about the underpants incident, but when she brings in the wicker hamper, I scan what's inside. It's got nothing but crisp white sheets in it. No stray underpants that I can see.

Mom lifts the first sheet out of the hamper, bringing the sheet to her nose as she takes hold of two corners. What Mom lacks in vision, she makes up for with her sense of smell. "Ahh," she says, "I challenge anyone who says there is a sweeter scent in all the world than sheets that have been drying on the line on a sunshiny day."

"You should write a poem about sheets!" Anne-Marie tells her.

"Maybe I shall."

Esther plops herself down in the middle of the sheet. "Okay, bounce me!"

When Mom and Anne-Marie each fold together their ends, the sheet becomes a makeshift hammock with Esther in it. When they bounce her, Esther laughs so hard the windows rattle. When I was little, Mom and Anne-Marie used to bounce me too. I wish I could remember how it felt.

Once the sheets are folded, I offer to bring them upstairs to the linen closet.

"Isaac, is everything all right in there?" I ask as I pass his room.

At first, Isaac doesn't answer. So I ask again.

"Every-*zing's* fine." His voice is flat.

"Did Granny have any news for you about your Tante Dora?" I hold my breath as I wait for Isaac's answer. Surely, he'd be crushed if he learned of Dora's death.

"No," he says from the other side of the door, "she doesn't mention Dora."

Later, when all of us are gathered around Granny's table for dinner, Dad opens Granny's letter. He uses Mom's silver letter opener, taking special care not to damage the stamp. Dad clears his throat before he begins to read.

Dearest children,

It gladdens my heart to imagine all of you seated at my old mahogany table, listening as my beloved son Martin reads you this letter. In a way, I feel as if I am with you all in Montreal.

I trust this letter finds you well. Here, things are as good as can be reasonably expected.

I'm glad for the vegetable garden I planted in the spring. It's produced enough onions and carrots and potatoes for me to share with the neighbours. Luxuries like coffee, sugar, and fresh eggs we are having to do without. Of course, we know we are far luckier than some.

It gladdens my heart to know that Isaac is with you, safe in the bosom of the Wolfson family's Canadian branch. It is mostly about Isaac that I am writing to you in today's letter. I have sent him a separate letter, which I trust he has received by now.

Without divulging its contents, I ask the rest of you one thing only: that you support Isaac as he begins to deal with the news I have shared with him.

Granddaughters, I conclude this letter by addressing you girls directly. I trust not only that you are doing your best at school and cooperating at home with your parents, each other, and your new brother but also that you continue to honor our Lord by attending synagogue and saying your prayers.

At my own advanced age, I will not be around for a great many more years, but it comforts me to no end to know that you girls and now Isaac, too, are carrying on the best of the Wolfson family's traditions.

With all my love always,
Granny

We all look over at Isaac. He is sitting perfectly still, his hands folded in his lap.

Esther breaks the silence. "I'm getting used to having a brother. Though it would be nice if he smiled more. And picked up his towels," she says, running her finger over her plate to collect the last of the crumbs from Anne-Marie's pudding *chômeur.* That's French for "unemployment, or poor man's cake." Anne-Marie told me the recipe, which calls for stale bread instead of flour, was invented during the Great Depression.

Esther's comments make Isaac blush. "I'll try to smile more," he says, without smiling. "And I'm sorry about the towels."

★ ★ ★

"It was a good letter," I tell Mom when, later, she comes to kiss us good night.

"Your Granny is a fine writer," Mom says, "with a strong voice."

"But I didn't like that bit about her not being around for a great many more years." The bedroom is dark, which somehow, makes this easier to say. Though she lives far away, I've always felt close to Granny.

Mom kisses my forehead. "That's just the kind of thing old people like to say. Granny is fit as a fiddle. And feisty too. In fact, Rosetta, of all of you, I've always felt you're the one who's most like her. And it isn't only the curls."

My heart swells when Mom says that. I'd love to become the sort of person Granny is: wise, unafraid to state her opinion, but always kind.

Mom has to cross under the butcher string to reach Annette's side of the room.

"What news do you think Granny shared with Isaac in the letter she wrote him?" I ask Mom.

Mom is kissing Annette's forehead, but when Mom is done, she turns to look at me. "We'll find that out when Isaac is ready to tell us. Until then, Rosetta, you're to respect his privacy."

Chapter 16

I adore the Ninth Floor at Eaton's.

It's the most elegant spot in Montreal, as elegant as the ballroom at the Ritz-Carlton Hotel. Only I've never actually been *inside* the ballroom. I only peeked at it when I've gone into the hotel with Dad to buy a magazine at the United Cigar Store inside or to use the ladies' bathroom when I have to pee too much to hold it in.

The funny thing is I don't even know if this restaurant is really named the Ninth Floor, though that's what everybody calls it. When there isn't a war going on, fancy fashion shows are held here every spring and fall. Models, some from as far away as Toronto and New York, parade down something called a catwalk, a runway set up down the middle of the restaurant. Annette says one day she'll be walking down the catwalk, modeling the latest fashions.

Even with a war going on, rich ladies still come to the Ninth Floor for tea (without sugar, mind you) or lunch after they have done their shopping. In fact, it was a very rich lady—Lady Flora McCrae Eaton, the wife of Sir John Craig Eaton, son of the department store's founder, Timothy Eaton—who came up with the design for the Ninth Floor.

Lady Flora wanted it to look just like the *Île de France*, a fancy French ocean liner she'd sailed on with her husband. So, to please his wife, Sir John hired a famous French architect named Jacques Carlu to design the dining room at the Montreal Eaton's branch.

I know all this because Miss Vipond is a fan of art deco. I like art deco, too, but what I like even more is the romantic story behind this elegant room. I have a feeling that despite her stern personality, Miss Vipond enjoys a good love story. I noticed how her eyes shone when she told us how Lady Flora was working as a nurse in Toronto when she first met Sir John, who was one of her patients. Lady Flora reminds me of a real-life Cinderella. Imagine having a husband who loves you so much—and who is so rich—that he can find a way to turn the inside of a restaurant into an ocean liner!

Sir John is the prince in the story, and Jacques Carlu is the fairy godfather! The thought of a fairy godfather carrying architectural plans instead of a magic wand makes me want to laugh out loud. Except there is no laughing out loud on the Ninth Floor. There is also no slurping, no raised voices and, definitely, no elbows on the table. When Esther's elbow drifts down toward the tablecloth, Mom gives her a sharp look, and the elbow returns to a more polite position.

I think we've come to the Ninth Floor today because Mom and Dad are trying to cheer Isaac up. He has been even quieter than usual (which is saying something) and taking even more of his solitary walks. We're also celebrating Esther's return to good health. She walked to synagogue last Saturday, though she had to stop for breaks, and later, during the rabbi's sermon, I caught her snoozing. To be honest, I dozed off too. Bertha had to wake me. She said I even snored a little!

"What do you think of those marble columns?" Dad asks Isaac. The two of them are sitting at one end of the table. Maybe it's because there are so many women at the Ninth Floor that the men feel they have to band together. (I've spotted two other men, also sitting huddled and a little out of place at the end of another table near ours.)

"Most impressive, sir, I mean Dad. That nave must be seven stories high."

Dad cranes his head to admire the nave. "A feat of engineering, if I say so myself."

We order tea and cucumber sandwiches. The sandwiches—tiny triangles of fluffy white bread with slivers of cucumber in between—arrive on a three-tiered stand with paper doilies on it. Our waiter wears a tuxedo and long white gloves. I don't think he's allowed to smile. Not even Esther, who giggles when he hands her a soft white napkin, can coax a smile out of him.

"May I ask whether you've ever considered a career in engineering?" Dad asks Isaac.

I know how much Isaac wants to be accepted into McGill's Medical School. Why on earth would he consider a career in engineering? And then, I see what Daddy is up to: he thinks that Isaac will not get into medical school, and he's trying to come up with some other plan. Even though I know Dad means well, what he's doing bothers me. Why can't

Isaac have his dream come true—the way Lady Flora's did?

"No, si . . . Dad, I haven't. It's medicine that interests me."

"Wasn't it Dr. Gordon who said it's always wise to have a contingency plan?" Annette says, joining the conversation. "You know, Isaac, engineering might just be your contingency plan."

I resist the urge to kick Annette under the table. Kicking your sister is also not allowed on the Ninth Floor.

"I've found life as an engineer to be most satisfying," Dad says. "And unlike a doctor, I've never met a bridge that required a house call—or a visit during the middle of the night."

Mom laughs and pats Dad's shoulder. I wish he would just drop this conversation. It's obvious from the way Isaac is fiddling with his napkin that he isn't enjoying himself.

"Rosetta," Annette nudges me with her elbow. "Are you feeling all right?"

"Yes . . . why do you ask?"

"Because this is the first time we've ever been at the Ninth Floor and you aren't eavesdropping on the conversations at some other table. It makes me think you're coming down with whatever Esther had." Annette puts her hand on my forehead to check my temperature.

"Will you sto—" I'm about to tell her not to be sarcastic, but then I realize she has a point. Two women at the next table are deep in conversation. Only I didn't notice them till now. I've been concentrating on the conversation at our own table. But I've learned that with someone like Annette, it's better to go on the attack, rather than try to defend myself. "Well," I say to her, "all you care about are women's hats and shoes."

Annette eyes the blouse I am wearing, one of her castoffs. "If you ask me, you'd benefit from becoming a little more interested in fashion."

"I didn't ask for your opinion," I hiss back. "Besides this blouse was good enough for you."

"Girls!" Mom and Dad say at the same time.

It's hard to enjoy cucumber sandwiches after that. Even when they come on a three-tiered platter.

Like a puppy, Esther can only sit still for so long. "Rosetta, can you take me for a walk?" she asks, her eyes going all puppy-dog hopeful too.

I say yes mainly because I need a break from Annette.

Isaac wants to come. I think he's had enough of admiring naves—and career advice.

The last person I expect to see in the menswear department is Mr. Schwartzberg. But there he is, standing over a bin of socks, when we walk down the stairs to the fifth floor. I would recognize those too-big trousers anywhere.

He spots me too. "Rosetta!" he calls out, sounding glad to see someone he knows.

I watch as his fox eyes land on Isaac, and for a moment, I worry Mr. Schwartzberg will say something about Isaac's Tante Dora.

I can feel my mind scrambling for some way to warn him not to give too much away.

But it's too late.

"Isaac, you are Isaac, aren't you?" Mr. Schwartzberg says, reaching for Isaac's hand and pumping it up and down. "Please allow me to offer my condolences about your Aunt Dora's d—"

Mr. Schwartzberg must notice the look in my eyes, because he stops short.

"Oh my God, no," Isaac whispers.

I try to reach for Isaac, but he has already fallen into the bin of socks.

Chapter 17

Pushing Isaac into talking doesn't work. Maybe pushing *anyone* into talking doesn't work. The problem is . . . well . . . I can be a little pushy.

I want to be kind to Isaac, but I also want to find out his story. If it wasn't Dora's death, and now I know for sure it wasn't, then what was the news Granny shared with him? I know Isaac has suffered—and still suffers—in ways I may never be able to understand. Isaac needs kindness. I want him to be happy, or at least not to be unhappy.

So I decide it's better not to knock on his door and ask whether he wants company or if he'd like to chat. When I do go with him on one of his walks, we walk quickly, too quickly for conversation. I think that for now, this is what Isaac needs.

As for me, I am getting used to quiet. Today the

only sound as we trudge up the path at Murray Hill Park is our breathing and the crunch of autumn leaves underneath our feet. The air smells smoky; with the October chill, Montrealers have begun using their fireplaces. I have to move quickly to keep up with Isaac because his legs are so much longer than mine. I want to tell Isaac that in a couple of months from now, we'll be tobogganing down this very hill. But I'm too out of breath to say a word.

It's become our routine to go for late afternoon walks. Isaac never asks me to join him. But when I hear him in the hallway, putting on his overcoat, I slip downstairs and head out with him. I've decided that the fact that he's never told me to go away means he likes my company. Unless, of course, it's because he's too polite—or too sad—to tell me to go away.

The Westmount maintenance crew has been out. They've raked up piles of leaves the size of small hills. We pass one by the tennis court.

I stop. That pile of leaves is calling to me, begging to be jumped in. At first, Isaac keeps walking. But when he turns around and spots me jumping on top of the pile, he stops. The leaves smell delicious— sweet and a little moldy because they've begun to rot—and I can feel leaf bits getting into my socks and shoes. Anne-Marie will have a fit if I track them into the house, but I don't care.

I'm watching Isaac's face, and for a moment, I think he's going to join me. But Isaac's too grown up and serious for jumping on leaves. He just stands and watches as I jump over and over again, flattening the pile. He is smiling. The smile makes his face look softer. I like to see him smile.

Isaac is also standing perfectly still, not walking in the mechanical way he has, his hands swinging close to his hips.

When I've had enough, I go back to him. I shake my head, and a few crisp leaf bits fall from my hair to the ground.

"I used to jump in the leaves *ven* I was small." Isaac's voice sounds almost rusty. "My mother vould take me to the park in Düsseldorf."

I don't say a word. I keep walking, matching my pace to Isaac's. Left foot forward, right foot follows, left then right, over and over again. I want him to tell me more. Isaac hasn't talked about his mother since the night he couldn't sleep and we had our chat in the kitchen.

"I remember the *pents* I used to wear to the park.

They had leather—how do you say in English?—suspenders. And I remember those little pieces of leaves, just like the ones that were in your hair just now, Rosetta. And I remember the sound of my mother's laughter. Like a bell." Something about the memory makes Isaac wince and walk more quickly. I don't understand why a happy memory upsets him, but I know I shouldn't ask.

"You know that letter that your granny wrote me?"

Isaac's voice is low, and for a moment, I wonder if my mind is playing tricks on me. Did he just mention Granny's letter—the one I've been so curious about—or was it the sound of the wind whistling through the thicket of maple trees?

"Yes," I whisper.

"The letter was about my mother."

"Your mother?" I turn around to face Isaac, and I'm afraid I've shouted. Why didn't I realize there might be news about Isaac's mother? "What did Granny have to say about your mother?" I've already broken my own rule and asked a question. And now that I've started, I've thought of another one. "Is she alive?"

Isaac takes hold of my forearm. "I can't keep up with you, Rosetta."

"Of course, you can. You're a much quicker walker than I am. It's your legs. They're much long—" Then I stop myself because I realize that isn't what Isaac means. I've asked him too many questions all at once.

I'm trying to decide which is the most important question and should come first, when Isaac begins to speak again. "My mother is alive." His voice sounds as if he hasn't decided if that is good or bad. "She contacted your granny."

"But isn't that good news? It means you're not an orphan after all!"

Isaac sucks in his breath, and I realize I shouldn't have used the word *orphan*. I'm remembering now, too, how he said his mother was dead to him—but he couldn't have meant it. Deep down, he must be glad to know she's alive. She is, after all, the only relative he has left.

"I know she gave you up," I say as gently as I can, "but if she's written to Granny, it must mean she wants to patch things up between the two of you. Have you written back to Granny?"

Isaac doesn't answer; he only shakes his head.

"But you must. She's your mother."

"There are other things about her," Isaac says,

"things I haven't told you." Isaac's words hang in the crisp air.

"What sorts of things?" Part of me is afraid to know the answer. Another part of me is curious. Is it better, I wonder again, to know or not to know? What if knowing changes everything? What then?

"My mother is very beautiful."

"I'm glad to hear it. But what do her looks have to do with anything?"

"You'll see," Isaac says. "If you can just listen and not keep interrupting the way you do."

"I didn't realize I was interrupting. I'm sorry, Isaac."

"There," he says, "you've done it again."

Chapter 18

The bench is my idea. It's not just because my calves are sore from keeping up with Isaac. He is taking me someplace very far and very sad, and I can almost feel the ground shifting under me, making me lose my balance. Sitting down helps steady me.

"My mother has the sort of looks the Nazis admire. Blonde hair—the same like Glynnis—a pale complexion and blue-blue eyes. She's tall too. Taller even *dan* me. For the Nazis, she's an Aryan goddess."

"An *Aryan* goddess?" I can't help interrupting again.

"Yes, Aryan." Isaac spits out the word. "The Nazis believe that Aryans are better *den* the rest of us. And that Jews and Gypsies are inferior and should be—" he pauses. I'm not sure whether the pause is meant to be dramatic, or if it's because telling me all this is so hard for him. "Eliminated."

The way he says *eliminated* makes me shiver. There's something so final about it. My mind flashes on the strip of fabric in Isaac's box. First, the Nazis would have to identify who was Jewish. If a person wears a yellow star he could be *eliminated*. Of course, I can't tell Isaac I've seen his yellow stars.

"Before the war," Isaac continues, "my mother worked in a milliner's shop, sewing lace and bows on wealthy women's hats. But the Nazis gave her a promotion." A dark look crosses Isaac's face when he says this. "*Dey* made her a teacher. She teaches Aryan *mädchen*—that's the German word for "girls"—how to be good Aryan wives and mothers."

My brain, which usually works quickly, is trying to make sense of what he's told me. I know it's wrong, evil even, to think that any group of people is inferior, but teaching women to be good wives and mothers, even Aryan ones, well, what's so wrong about that?

"You don't understand, do you?" Isaac raises his voice, and for a moment, I think he blames me for whatever his mother has done.

"I want to be a wife and mother someday," I stammer. It's all I can think of saying.

Isaac rubs his temples. "Perhaps I need to explain *tings* better. The *mädchen* who go to *dees* schools don't learn math or science. They don't take part in public speaking contests." Isaac watches me when he says this. "They learn how to roast a chicken and sew a hem." I don't say what I am thinking—there's no crime in roasting a chicken or sewing a hem.

"But that's not all my mother teaches the *mädchen*." Isaac closes his eyes the way he does when he is remembering. When he opens them, I can't tell where he is—sitting next to me on a bench in Murray Hill Park, or back in Düsseldorf.

"I hadn't heard from her in *veeks*," he says, "months even. It was after she first left me with Tante Dora. I was still getting used to *tings*. Tante Dora was always kind, but she wasn't my mother. My mother wasn't perfect, but I was used to her. In those first *veeks* and months, I missed her *some-ting* terrible."

"Tante Dora was the one who let the news slip out. She heard Mother was teaching at the *mädchen's* school. So, one afternoon, I *vent der*."

"The school was in *dees* beautiful gray brick house that once belonged to the Fraenkels, a wealthy Jewish family. When the Nazis took over, they confiscated Jewish people's houses—along with *every-ting* that belonged to them, their possessions, their businesses, *every-ting*. The Fraenkels had nowhere to go." The memory makes Isaac sigh.

"What about your Tante Dora? Did they take her things away too?"

"Tante Dora thought ahead. Luckily, she *vas* close with Hilde, the Christian woman who *vas* her housekeeper for many years. They were like sisters. Tante Dora transferred the deed of her apartment to Hilde. That meant we could continue living in the apartment. Now where *vas* I in my story?"

"You were telling me about the day you went to see your mother at the *mädchen's* school."

"Yes, that's right. It's a day I'll never forget, because *every-ting* changed for me *zat* day. I was standing on the porch. Through a *vindow*, I could see my mother at the front of a classroom, behind a row of sewing machines. Her students were at their desks, watching my mother. She was holding a long wooden pointer, to direct the *mädchen* to a poster."

"My mother was so busy she didn't see me peering through the window. First, I thought the poster was for a biology class. There were half a dozen noses and pairs of eyes on *zat* poster. But then I heard my mother's voice, so strong I could hear it from outside. '*Mädchen*,' she said, 'It is essential that you are able to identify the characteristics of a Jew.' I'll never forget the way she said 'Jew.' Like she had smelled sour milk."

"'Here you have,' my mother continued, 'four Jewish noses—long and pointed and very ugly. And here you have two pairs of Jewish eyes. See how dark and mean they are.'"

Isaac's story is making me feel sick to my stomach.

Isaac looks down at his feet. "I thought of my father. The Jew she married. Because I was so young when he died, I don't remember his face. I don't remember his nose or his eyes. I only remember his hands. His hands . . . were always warm." Isaac makes a gulping sound.

"You know what, Rosetta? At that moment, for the first time in my life, I was glad my father *vas* dead." Isaac sucks in his breath. "At least he never knew what kind of monster his wife was."

Because I don't know what else to do, I shake my head. I've always considered Glynnis's mother a nuisance for worrying too much, and I sometimes feel annoyed by how my mother disappears into her poems, but this—what Isaac is telling me now—is worse than anything I ever imagined. His mother teaches hatred! And by betraying the memory of Isaac's father, she has betrayed Isaac too. No wonder he's so angry. Not just at her, but at the world. And at God Himself.

"Oh, Isaac," I say, "I'm so sorry."

Isaac doesn't want my sympathy. He gets up from the bench. Then he crosses his arms over his chest and sighs. "I still haven't told you the worst of it," he whispers.

But this is all Isaac will tell me, at least for today. To be honest, I'm relieved. I don't know how much more of his story I can take. My heart feels like it's breaking just from imagining what Isaac has described. What must *his* heart feel like?

I get up from the bench too. Again, I have the feeling the ground is shifting under me. There is nothing I can say to comfort Isaac, or if there is, I'm not smart enough to think of it. All I can do is keep walking by his side as we make our way up to Westmount Avenue and then back to Argyle.

Chapter 19

Everything smells like apples—sharp, sweet, and fresh—the air, my fingers, and even Esther's hair when I lift her up so she can pick her own apple.

We come to Mont St. Hilaire every year, always on a Sunday before the frost sets in and always to Vergers Duval because Mom and Dad say Monsieur Duval's apples are the nicest.

We each fill a basket with McIntosh or Empire apples that Mom will store in the cellar. We'll have apples to eat all winter long (though by the end of winter, the McIntosh apples will lose their crunch and taste a little mealy) and plenty of Empires left over for Mom and Anne-Marie's applesauce and apple jelly. Because it's canning season, the Canadian government has temporarily increased our sugar rations. Mom says that come February, a little apple jelly spread on toast gives a person courage to last till spring.

Mom and Dad insist we pick in pairs. That's so one of us can keep the wooden stepladder steady—Monsieur Duval supplies the ladders—while the other climbs up into the tree and snaps the apples loose. The trick is to grab the bottom of the apple and twist a little in order to loosen the stem along with the fruit.

I shouldn't have worn patent leather pumps. But ever since Annette criticized my clothing, I've been paying more attention to how I dress. The pumps are my favorite hand-me-downs ever. They are still in good condition because Annette outgrew them before the season was over. The others are wearing rubber boots, which I'll admit is more sensible, especially since the ground is muddy. If I step too hard, my heels sink into it.

"Are you sure that's a good idea?" Mom said when she noticed me slipping on the pumps.

"I'll be careful," I told her. And probably because she was busy preparing for our outing, Mom didn't say more about my shoes. To be honest, I am getting a little worried about my pumps. The mud might leave stains.

Annette chose Isaac for her picking partner. They are at a tree just down the row from the one where Esther and I are working. Annette is holding the ladder, and I can hear her bossing Isaac: "You've missed one. Up and to the left. And there's another near it. Get that one too! To the left I told you!"

Isaac is going to get a stiff neck from the gymnastics Annette is forcing him to do!

Esther squawks when I put her down. "No, no! I want to pick more!" Her cheeks are as red as apples.

I point to some of the apples that have fallen to the ground. "What about those?"

"They're wormy!" Esther says, wriggling her body like a worm.

"Not all of them," I tell her. "The wind brought some of those apples down. Some people say windfall apples are the best tasting. But we'll need to inspect them for bruises." I pick up an apple from the ground to demonstrate. "Look, this one's perfect."

Esther inspects the apple, too, and soon, she is scouring the grass, looking for windfall.

Monsieur Duval is repairing the wooden fence that surrounds the orchard. He is wearing blue jeans and a red-and-black lumber shirt.

"Are you taking us for a tractor ride?" Esther calls out to him.

I've always liked tractor rides, but I'm worried about my shoes.

Monsieur Duval puts down his hammer and wipes the sweat from his forehead. "*Peut-être*," he says. "Maybe. But only if you let me finish my work first."

"What are you working on?" Esther asks him.

"See this hole?" he says. "If I don't fix it, deer could get into the orchard this winter."

"Oh, I love deer! They're so pretty," Esther says.

"They might be pretty. But they eat bark. And that can kill an apple tree," Monsieur Duval says.

"After you fix the fence, will you take us, then?" Esther asks.

"Eddie, I hope you're not being a nuisance," Dad says. He and Mom have walked over to where we are. Annette and Isaac have come too.

"Monsieur Duval doesn't like deer," Esther says.

"I was just saying I'd take the children for a tractor ride. Only I need to finish fixing this fence. And then I have to do some pruning," Monsieur Duval tells Dad.

"Mom says prunes help with diges—" Esther can't get the word out.

"Digestion!" Annette says sharply.

"I was speaking of prunes," Mom explains, blushing a little, "not pruning."

"I see," Monsieur Duval says. "Spring is the best time for heavy pruning. But this time of year, I like to do some light pruning. So the trees will harden."

"Harden?" I ask.

"Yes, harden," Monsieur Duval says, and I think he likes being able to talk about trees. "Trees are like people. We need to be tough—we need to be hard—to withstand the harshest conditions."

"How true!" Dad says.

Mom doesn't look so convinced. "With people at least, too hard isn't always a good thing."

Am I imagining it, or does Mom glance at Isaac when she says that?

Chapter 20

Annette says she's too grown up for tractors. "And by the way, so are you!" she tells Isaac, wagging her finger in front of his nose. "Besides, wouldn't you rather join me for a walk?"

Isaac says that though a walk sounds nice, he's never been on a tractor.

"Have it your way, then," Annette says in a way that makes me think she'd rather have it her way.

"Well, then, Son," Dad claps Isaac on the shoulder, "you'd better hop on. I'm pleased to see you've got an interest in machinery. I'm a civil engineer myself, but you could do worse than to take up a career in mechanical engineering."

Wanting to save Isaac from more career advice, I tug on his sleeve. "Let's go," I tell him. "There's room for two on the back of Monsieur Duval's tractor."

"I want to sit up front with Monsieur Duval!" Esther calls out.

About three minutes later, Isaac and I are sitting on the back of the tractor, the breeze in our hair, our legs stretched out in front of us. "Do you like my shoes?" I ask Isaac.

"They're very elegant. They'd be even nicer without the mud."

"Why, Isaac! I think you just made a joke!"

Though the sky is mostly blue, there are some clouds with ash-colored edges. The air has that heavy feeling it gets before a rain shower. Hopefully, that won't happen till we're back in the car, headed home.

Monsieur Duval takes us over a large bump, and Isaac and I are lifted momentarily from our seats.

Esther's giggling sounds like music.

I've stuffed two McIntosh apples into my pockets, and now I polish one on my skirt and pass it to Isaac. Then I polish the other and bite into it. It has the sweet crispness the first apple of the season always does. No apple will taste this delicious until we return to the orchard next fall.

"You're from *à travers de l'océan*, across the ocean, aren't you?" Monsieur Duval calls out. "I heard your accent back there."

"Yes," Isaac calls back, "I'm from Düsseldorf, Germany."

"What's it like over there?" Monsieur Duval asks.

"It used to be beautiful. But no more. The whole country—the whole continent—has gone insane. Canada is a much better place."

"I know a little about what's going on overseas. Even apple farmers like me hear things. But I'll tell you youngsters one thing: I don't see why our Canadian boys have to cross the ocean to fight your battles. I hope you won't take that in the wrong way, young man. *C'est ce que je pense.* It's just what I think."

I'm half expecting Isaac to get angry, the way he did on the rowboat with Broderick, but he doesn't. He just sighs. "This battle's too big," Isaac pauses to choose his words, "and too ugly . . . for Europe to fight on its own. If Hitler gets his way, why, he'll take over the world."

It scares me when Isaac says that. I never imagined that Hitler could bring his war across the ocean!

Then, instead of finishing his apple the way I'm finishing mine, eating it down to the core until there is nothing left but a few black seeds, Isaac throws his—hard—to the ground.

Monsieur Duval seems to have had enough conversation. But Isaac's still in the mood to talk. "Are you ready for the rest of my story now, Rosetta?"

"If you're ready to tell it, I'm ready to listen."

Isaac must like my answer, because for a moment, his face relaxes. "You probably think it's bad enough that my mother teaches hatred at the *mädchen's* school."

I nod my head. "Yes, I think it's bad and also sad."

"Sad for me, certainly," Isaac says. "But I'm finished with feeling sad. My anger is bigger than my sadness."

There Isaac goes again—thinking his way of looking at things is the only way. "Sad for her too," I whisper.

"Bah," Isaac waves his hand in front of him as if he'd like to wave away my words. "Not sad for her at all. She's the sort of person who knows how to look out for herself. Even if she didn't look out for me."

"Maybe she couldn't. Or maybe she did the best she could."

"Bah," Isaac says again, and this time, the *Bah* sounds like a growl. "Why don't I tell you the rest of the story? Then you decide what you think of my mother." He says the word *mother* as if he is talking about a table or a chair, not a person.

"Remember that afternoon I told you about? When I went to the *mädchen's* school? I could have left when I saw her pointing at that disgusting poster. But I didn't. *Some-ting* made me stay. The class was still in session.

'*Mädchen*,' I heard my mother say. She laid her pointer stick on the desk and looked up at her students. 'Your destiny—your contribution to the cause—is to find a suitable husband—an Aryan husband. A man who is tall, with blond hair and blue eyes. A man who supports the Nazi Party. Together, you will further the cause by creating a new generation of Nazis.' Her eyes were lit up as if she was possessed."

"Then one of the *mädchen* turned her head to look out the window—maybe she was imagining her Aryan husband—and she spotted me outside. The *mädchen* shrieked. Maybe she was comparing my nose and eyes with the ones on the poster. The other *mädchen* shrieked too. My mother rushed to the window.

Our eyes met. But when she looked at me, Rosetta, it was as if I was a stranger. Rosetta, she hadn't seen me in months! I *vas* her only child.

'*Verloren gehen!*' she yelled. 'Get lost! If you don't go now, I'll call the police!' Her gray-blue eyes were flat. I was nothing to her. No, less than nothing."

I put my hand in front of my mouth. Because I don't know what to say, I don't say anything at all.

Isaac looks at me. "Do you understand, now, Rosetta, why I can't bring myself to write to her?"

The rain is coming down harder. Monsieur Duval picks up speed. Isaac's cheeks are soaked. I know it isn't only from the rain.

Chapter 21

Isaac's story is like a knapsack. It has weighed me down since he began telling it to me. With each addition, my knapsack gets heavier and harder to carry. It's with me in the morning, when I wake up, and it's never far from my mind during the day. Even when I close my eyes to sleep, I see a tall blonde woman pointing with her stick to the hideous poster, then looking through the window at her only child as if he were a stranger.

At school, when I should be concentrating on Miss Vipond's Latin lesson, I think about Isaac's mother. I wish I could talk to Mom and Dad, see what advice they might have for me and Isaac, but I can't. They'll say, "We told you not to bring up the subject of the war. We explained that Isaac needs time." And what will I answer? That I forced the story out of him or that he needed to tell someone and that that someone happened to be me?

From outside the classroom, I hear a siren's piercing screech. Some of the boys get up from their desks to look out the window.

"Do you think it's a fire?" Gerald O'Shaughnessy asks excitedly.

Miss Vipond claps her hands. "Away from the windows, boys! Now!" she says, raising her voice. "That siren is an 'all-clear signal.' We're having an Air Raid Precautions practice. All of you under your desks, crouched with your heads down, this instant!"

We scramble for cover, and except for our breathing, the room falls silent. Even Gerald O'Shaughnessy seems, for once, to have nothing to say. Miss Vipond is under her desk, too, one eye on the class, the other on her watch. She's explained that each teacher has to keep a record of how long the exercise takes. Those numbers will be submitted to the principal, Mr. Owen, who will submit them to the city's Air Raid Precautions Committee.

Dad says there is no need to worry, that a war can't travel across an ocean. But as we crouch under our desks, our arms cradling our heads, I can't help worrying. The war is already traveling across the European continent like a wildfire that can't be stopped. According to the *Gazette*, the Nazis are preparing to invade Russia again—they're even building special heaters to help them withstand the Russian winter. What if Hitler manages to conquer all Europe—and what if, if he does, that is not enough for him? What if he wants to conquer the whole world?

Last period, there's a special school-wide assembly. Mr. Owen stands by the entrance to the gym as we file in. Gerald O'Shaughnessy slinks past him. Mr. Owen gave Gerald the strap last year for swearing.

"Boys and girls," Mr. Owen says when we are all seated, cross-legged, on the gym floor. "I've called you here today to let you know the results from this morning's Air Raid Precautions practice are not very good. According to the numbers I've seen, it took some of you nearly four minutes—four minutes!— to get into position underneath your desks. Which is why I've decided, in conjunction with Monsieur Letourneau, your physical education teacher, to take action. Instead of playing tag and badminton and floor hockey during your phys ed classes, there will be a new focus." When some of the boys make groaning sounds, Mr. Owen gives us all a stern look. "You'll be running and jumping and throwing. And Monsieur Letourneau," Mr. Owen looks over to the side of the room and nods at Monsieur Letourneau, "will be timing you. Our goal is for all of you to improve your physical conditioning so that when the next Air Raid Precautions practice takes place, you'll be far quicker than you were today."

Mr. Owen stops to adjust his glasses, which have slipped down his nose during his speech. "Before dismissing you, boys and girls, I want you to remember that this new program is for your own good. And for the good of our fine country and the values for which it stands."

* * *

"There's chalk on your skirt, Miss," I tell my teacher.

Miss Vipond gets up from her chair and shakes her skirt clean. Tiny chalk particles drift down to the linoleum floor. "Have you stayed this afternoon just to tell me that, Rosetta? And where's Glynnis? I rarely have the pleasure of seeing one of you without the other."

"I told her I wanted to talk to you about my public speaking."

"I see." Miss Vipond's eyes look warmer than they do when she is giving us Latin lessons. "Well, by all means, go ahead then."

"Uh . . ." I feel the color rising to my cheeks. "Only that isn't really what I want to talk to you about. I want to talk to you about Isaac . . . the boy who's come to live with us, my new brother."

"Why don't you have a seat, then, Rosetta? And would you like a cookie?"

To my surprise, Miss Vipond takes out a small cookie tin from her top drawer and offers me one. It tastes a little stale.

"What is it you want to tell me about your brother?"

"Well . . ." Now that I finally have a chance to talk to someone about Isaac's story, I hardly know where to begin. There's so much to tell, and it's all so complicated. I decide to start with the most important part. "He hates his mother."

"Hates her?" Miss Vipond furrows her brow. "Why, that's very unfortunate."

"Isaac told me things about her and now, I'm beginning to hate her too. She doesn't sound like a very nice person or a very good mother."

Miss Vipond has been rolling her pencil along her blotter, but now she puts two fingers down on the pencil to stop it from moving. "What sorts of things did Isaac tell you?"

I grip the bottom of my chair. "Well . . . first, I should explain that Isaac's mother isn't Jewish. She's been working in a Nazi school, teaching young German girls to be good Aryan wives and mothers and," I stop to take a breath, "to hate Jews."

Miss Vipond bites her lip. "That does sound very bad."

"Oh, Miss Vipond, it's terrible. And now she's found a way to contact my granny in England and . . . she . . . she wants to resume contact with Isaac. She gave him up—because he's half Jewish. Well, as you might expect, he doesn't want to write to her and I don't know what to advise him."

"Advise him?" Miss Vipond raises her eyebrows. "Has Isaac asked for your advice?"

"Not exactly. But I know he wants it. Why else would he have told me?"

"Sometimes," Miss Vipond says softly, "a person just wants to tell his story. To get it out."

"Even so. Isaac needs advice. And I don't know what to tell him."

"There's something I'm curious about Rosetta." Miss Vipond looks up at me. "Why have you come to me—and not your parents?"

"They'll think I wheedled the story out of him. And honestly, Miss Vipond, I didn't. Though I do admit I was curious. Very curious, even. My parents say we mustn't say anything to remind Isaac of his past. 'Give him time,'" I say in what sounds to my ears like a decent imitation of my mom.

"I can understand that sentiment," Miss Vipond says, nodding her head. "Sometimes it's best not to scratch at a sore."

For a moment, I'm worried that now Miss Vipond will be upset with me too. But then she gives me a tight-lipped smile. "On the other hand," she says, "sometimes I think bottling things up can make them worse. Bigger even than they were."

"Oh, I'm so glad you feel that way, Miss Vipond. Because as I said before, I *have* been curious to know Isaac's story. I read the *Gazette* every morning, but honestly, they say so little about the dreadful things that are happening to European Jews. I agree it's important we know about Canadian casualties, but surely, there's more we need to know. So, Miss Vipond, if Isaac does ask my advice—and I'm sure he will—what do I tell him? Should he write back to his mother, or should he just continue to pretend she's dead, the way he has been doing?"

Miss Vipond has picked up her pencil and is tapping her chin with the eraser. "I wonder what Isaac's mother would have to say in her own defense. Has it occurred to you, Rosetta—and to Isaac—that perhaps in some twisted way, his mother is trying to help him? I can't imagine a mother *not* trying to help her child."

"But she gave him up," I sputter, "because he was a Jew."

"But he's safe now, isn't he?" Miss Vipond asks.

"That has nothing to do with his mother!" I say. Why is Miss Vipond being so blind?

"Are you quite sure of that, Rosetta?"

"Of course I'm sure." But inside, I'm less sure than I sound. "Don't you think it's possible Isaac's mother might be entirely evil?"

Miss Vipond stiffens when I say that. "Personally, I don't think anyone is entirely—irredeemably—evil. I also believe strongly in reconciliation, whenever it is possible."

Miss Vipond folds her hands in her lap as if to say she's pleased with the points she has made. "You've been learning about human nature in your English class, haven't you? Shakespeare's Macbeth, for instance, wasn't entirely evil. Ambitious, yes, greedy, most definitely, but not irredeemably evil—despite his crimes."

I'm still not convinced. How could Isaac's mother teach girls to hate Jews when her own husband—the man she loved—was a Jew? Then I think of something else. "What about Hitler? Isn't he irredeemably evil?"

Miss Vipond bites down hard on her lower lip. She seems to have no answer for that.

Chapter 22

Mom's eyes are getting worse. Her magnifying loupe is not strong enough. "Maybe I need a new one," she tells Dad when he comes in after work and finds her at her desk in the parlor, struggling to read a poem by Sir Alfred Tennyson, who is one of Mom's heroes.

"I think it's time to see a specialist, dear," Dad says.

Mom sighs. "I suppose you're right—though I don't think there's much anyone will be able to do. My mother's eyes got worse and worse, and by the time she was sixty, she was nearly blind. Let's hope the girls have inherited *your* eyes, Martin."

Dad strokes Mom's shoulder. "We'll need to find an ophthalmologist. Surely something can be done. We could even go to New York for a consult."

Mom looks into Dad's eyes and takes his hand in hers. "If, one day, I do lose my sight altogether—and

I know it's possible despite all the positive thinking in the world—I will always remember your kind face."

"Oh, Mom, don't talk like that!" I say, from my spot on the sofa, where I have been gobbling up *Little Women* by Louisa May Alcott. "Besides, if you do take after your mother, you've got another twenty years before you go mostly blind."

"You make a good point, Rosetta," Dad tells me as he gives me a stern look, "though you might have found a gentler way to express it."

"I only meant—"

Mom looks up from her poetry book. Her eyes do look very tired. "Never mind, Rosetta. Besides, you're right, I have loads of time. It's just that once you're a grown-up, time passes so quickly. It feels like not too long ago I was twelve myself."

Annette has come downstairs. "I'm a grown-up, or very nearly," she says haughtily. "If you ask me, time doesn't pass nearly quickly enough. I can't wait till I'm old enough to become a fashion model and have a house of my own. Then I won't have to share my room with Ros—"

She stops herself when she notices Isaac is in the parlor, too, standing behind Dad. "Oh, Isaac, I thought you were out on one of your walks."

"Isaac spent the day with me at the office," Dad says. He is trying to make the awkward moment a little less awkward.

"How was it?" I ask Isaac. I'm sure the invitation was part of Dad's plan to get Isaac interested in engineering.

"Just fine." Isaac answers too quickly. Then he turns to Mom. "Was there mail for me today?"

"As a matter of fact, there was something." Mom opens the top drawer of her desk and takes out an envelope. I recognize the red McGill crest in the left corner. Even my heart is thumping fast.

Isaac grabs the letter from Mom's hand. Then he turns to head upstairs. We're all watching him, holding our breath.

Esther lifts her head. She's been lying in front of the fireplace, playing with her bunny. "Can't you open it here? With us?" she asks Isaac. "Please!"

Dad and Mom exchange a nervous look. I can tell they are communicating without words, trying to decide which of them will say something. Mom blinks so quickly I'm not even sure it happened, but it seems to be the signal for Dad to speak.

"Isaac would probably prefer a little privacy right now, dear," he tells Esther. "Son, go on upstairs and open your letter in your own room. You can tell us about it afterward or whenever you feel ready to discuss it. There's absolutely no rush, of course. You must take whatever time you need."

To my surprise, Isaac reaches for Mom's silver letter opener and slits the envelope open then and there. He takes out the letter and unfolds it. His fingers are trembling the way mine did the day of the public speaking competition. I watch his dark eyes fly over the letter.

His face gives nothing away. He does not smile or scowl.

"Well, what does it say?" Oh my, I've gone ahead and blurted it out. But I couldn't stop myself. I'm so eager to know whether Isaac has been accepted into the Faculty of Medicine. So many sad things have happened to him, surely he, of all people, deserves to get some good news.

"How rude of you to ask him that!" Annette says, looking at me as if I'd robbed the Royal Bank.

"How rude of you to complain about having to share your room!"

"You're the worst person to share with. You're always leaving your things on my side of the butcher string."

"Who ever heard of dividing a room with butcher string?"

"Girls, stop it *now*!" Dad says.

Isaac clears his throat. "It appears the Faculty of Medicine has put me on its waiting list." His voice is as neutral as his face.

"Why, that's excellent news!" Dad says, clapping his hands together.

Only there is something hollow about the sound of his clapping.

Esther sighs. "That means Isaac didn't get in, doesn't it?"

"Not at all, dear," Mom tells Esther, but she turns to look at Isaac too. "It means there's hope."

"Well, then," I say, jumping up from my spot to go and shake Isaac's hand. "Dad is right. This is excellent news. Or at least good news."

Isaac shakes my hand, but it's not hard to see his heart isn't in it. "I've learned," he mutters under his breath, "that hope can be a dangerous thing."

★ ★ ★

Isaac doesn't feel like going for a walk, either before dinner or after dinner. He says the day at Dad's office has worn him out and he needs a nap. But when I hear noises coming from my old room, I know Isaac isn't napping. I also know from the way he's closed the door—not leaving it open even a crack—that he is not in the mood for conversation, not even with me. Even if Isaac has never said so, I know I'm his favorite sister. After all, I'm his walking companion, not to mention the only one who knows his story.

I'm still thinking over what Isaac said about hope. That hope can be dangerous. I always thought hope was good—and necessary. We all hoped Esther would recover and she did. Annette hopes one day she will be a fashion model with a home of her own. (I hope that too.) Dad and Mom are hopeful an ophthalmologist will be able to save Mom's vision. There's no danger in hoping. Or is there? What if a person hopes for something that will never ever happen? What if Europe's Jews hoped the Nazis would let them be, but the Nazis came after them all the same, forcing them to wear yellow stars and rounding them up into cattle cars the way Mr. Schwartzberg described? Maybe in those cases, hope blinded people from the truth: that they were running out of time. And that's a kind of blindness no eye specialist—not even one in New York—can fix. Maybe that is what Isaac meant.

I hear him open the closet door in my old room. Perhaps he is putting away the letter or saving the stamp for his collection.

If only there was something I could do to improve Isaac's chances of getting into medical school. Maybe I could talk to Mr. Benbow, plead Isaac's case. But I know Isaac wouldn't want that, especially considering how he feels about Broderick.

I hear scuffling sounds coming from inside the closet. What is going on in there?

Now I hear quick footsteps and the door to my old bedroom clicking open.

"Rosetta!" Isaac calls out. His voice sounds sharp, as if he's having trouble holding in his anger. At first, I think it has something to do with his being on the waiting list. But, of course, I have nothing to do with any of that.

I get up from my bed where I've been lying and walk out to the hallway. Isaac is standing in his doorway. "Rosetta!" he says again. "Have you been inside my closet?"

"No," I answer automatically, crossing my arms over my chest. Isaac's eyes burn as he watches my face. "Well, only once. To get the snakes and ladders board for Esther, when she was still too weak to get up from the couch. You remember how weak she was, don't you, Isaac?"

Is that sweat on Isaac's brow?

"Besides," I tell him, "it's *my* closet, not yours." I stamp my foot for effect. I feel as if Isaac is the bull and I'm the Spanish matador. If Isaac is angry with me, why then, I'll be angry with him. We'll see who has the stronger personality!

"Rosetta!"

"Will you stop calling me 'Rosetta' like that!" And now I see that Isaac is holding something between his fingers. It's the orange-yellow fabric with the Jewish stars on it. So that's why he's so upset!

My brain is tap dancing in my head as it tries to come up with some explanation or excuse. *It wasn't me who went through your closet. It must have been Esther, you know how she gets when she's looking for her bunny. Or else it was Anne-Marie when she was dusting. There's nothing Anne-Marie likes more than dusting the hard-to-reach spots. I've never seen that strip of fabric in all my life! Besides, I have better things to do than poke inside other people's closets. What sort of person do you take me for, anyhow?*

But I can see from Isaac's face there is no point in inventing stories. He knows it was me. I know, too, how private Isaac is.

I unfold my arms. "I . . . I was curious," I tell him.

"You found these, didn't you?" Isaac unfurls the fabric and waves the stars in front of me. His voice is angrier than ever.

I see the top of Dad's balding head coming up the stairs. *Oh no!* I think to myself.

"Is there something going on up here?" Dad asks. "Some problem I should know about?" Dad looks from Isaac to me, then back to Isaac. Isaac has put his hands behind his back so there's no sign of the orange-yellow fabric. "Isaac—Son—is something wrong? Rosetta, what's going on up here?"

"It's nothing," I say. "Or at least nothing we can't mend on our own."

"Is that true, Son?" Dad lays his hand on Isaac's shoulder. It bothers me that without knowing anything at all about our argument, Dad is taking Isaac's side. I'm his daughter after all. His *real* daughter. Because even if he just called Isaac *Son*, Isaac isn't Dad and Mom's *real* son. Just as he isn't my *real* brother. Even if he lives with us till he's a hundred years old, he will never really be a member of our family! "Isaac," Dad asks. "Has Rosetta been snooping again?"

I hope Dad doesn't notice my cheeks redden. "Well, has she?" Dad asks again.

I keep my eyes planted on the wooden floorboards. If I look at Dad, I'm afraid I'll give myself away.

When Isaac speaks, his voice is no longer sharp. "As Rosetta said, this is something we can mend on our own. And I'm sorry, Dad, if we disturbed you."

It's only when I hear Isaac apologize to Dad that I realize I haven't apologized to Isaac. I've tried making an excuse, I've tried getting angry at him, but I haven't apologized. I can fix that. I'll apologize the minute Dad goes downstairs.

Only Isaac doesn't give me a chance. The moment Dad turns his back, Isaac goes back to his room. He doesn't look in my direction or say a single word to me. As I stand at the door to the bedroom I'm sharing with Annette, I can't help thinking that even being shouted at would feel better than this.

Chapter 23

Mom says there's an art to apologizing. The person who is apologizing should not make excuses. If he or she does, it is not, according to Mom, a real apology. I try to keep that advice in mind as I write my note to Isaac.

I know there's no point in knocking on his door. Isaac is too upset to talk to me. Better to slide my note under the door and then when he's ready, he'll read it. And forgive me, of course.

Dear Isaac,

I'm deeply sorry for invading your privacy and also for hurting your feelings. But I didn't realize how much those Jewish stars meant to you.

I shouldn't have said *"but."* That's making an excuse. So I start again.

> *Dear Isaac,*
> *I'm deeply sorry for invading your privacy and also for hurting your feelings. I can't seem to control my snoopy nature.*

That part about my snoopy nature is another excuse. This note is no good either. I crumple it up and toss it into the wastepaper basket.

> *Dear Isaac,*
> *I'm deeply sorry for invading your privacy and also for hurting your feelings. I hope that you will find it in your heart to forgive me. Our friendship means a lot to me.*
> *Yours,*
> *Rosetta*

I read the note over (twice) and decide this one works. Just as I'm folding it in three, I hear footsteps in the hallway, and a moment later, a folded sheet of paper comes sliding under my door.

I don't move from my chair. When I look down

at the letter, I recognize Isaac's cramped handwriting. What a coincidence that he has been writing to me at almost the very second I was writing to him. It feels almost spooky. I am tempted to shoot right out of my room and tell Isaac this, but in the end, I don't. I wait until Isaac's door clicks shut, only then instead of reading his letter right away, I slide the letter I have written to him under his door. This way, he will see the coincidence too. That will help soften his feelings and make him more open to accepting my apology.

Though I haven't known Isaac long, the idea of not being close with him, of no longer being his confidante, hurts me more than I would have expected. So this is what it feels like to have a brother.

Something about Isaac's handwriting strikes me as sad. Maybe it's the crampedness, as if he feels he must use every inch of the sheet, and not waste any open space. It's tidy, too, almost too tidy, as if it was written by a machine, not a person.

Dear Rosetta,

It's easier for me to express these thoughts in writing, which is why I am writing this letter to you.

For reasons I do not fully understand, you're the sister to whom I feel closest. The one whose company I most enjoy.

I flush with pride when I read this part. Isaac *enjoys* my *company*. I can't wait to tell Annette! She'll be green with envy!

Only then, I feel a guilty pit in my stomach. If I'm the sister to whom Isaac feels closest, the one whose company he most enjoys, why then, if I've hurt or betrayed him in some way, that must make him feel even worse.

Perhaps that is why what you've done by going into my closet and opening up my private carton has left me feeling so hurt and exposed.

So I was right about how much I've hurt him. Part of me wants to stop reading his letter right now. Another part of me wants to know more.

Rosetta, I have told you a great deal—perhaps too much—about my history. It isn't that you pried it out of me, rather it's that I felt comfortable enough with you to share my story. But those Jewish stars, the ones I keep in the box at the very back of the closet, those are a different matter. I have not been able to look at them since I packed them away in Düsseldorf.

As painful as they are to me, those stars are important. They tell the truth. They are the only proof I have of what is happening in Germany, and elsewhere in Europe.

Maybe now you will understand better why I got so angry. I suppose I'm a little like a wounded animal. I need time to like my wounds.

Yours,

Isaac

Like my wounds? Isaac must have meant to say *Lick my wounds.* I take another look at the letter. Was I reading too quickly? No, that is what it says. *Like my wounds.* I repeat the words under my breath. Isaac has made a mistake, but what an interesting mistake it is!

Chapter 24

Esther saw Dr. Gordon for a check-up. He said she may keep exercising, but she shouldn't overdo it. He suggested she go swimming at the Westmount YMCA, which is only a few blocks from our house.

"Swimming works all the major muscles, including the heart. Did you know the heart was a muscle, Esther?" Dr. Gordon asks. I heard all this even though I was outside, sitting in the waiting room. Either Dr. Gordon has a very loud voice or else the walls at his office are paper thin—either way, it's excellent for listening in. Imagine if Dr. Gordon was having a more private conversation, if, say, he was giving advice to a patient who was depressed. ("Perhaps you could tell me, dear, why you're feeling so blue? Has your heart been broken?

If it has, it might help to tell me about it . . .") My spine tingles at the thought of listening in on that sort of conversation.

Because Mom wants to encourage not only Esther's swimming, but all of ours, she bought us all new swimsuits at Simpson's, where the summer stock was on sale.

"I'd have preferred to choose my own," Annette said when she saw that Mom had picked out the same blue-and-white-striped suit for each of us. "I'd have chosen an all black one."

"Look at the bright side," I said, "we'll be mostly underwater when we wear them."

Esther takes a private swim lesson at 11 a.m. on Sundays. The rest of us join her in the pool a half hour later at free swim. I'm extra excited today, not just because I like splashing and practicing my strokes but because Glynnis is coming too.

Glynnis and Broderick have had breakfast with their parents at the Murrays' on Sherbrooke Street. When Glynnis meets up with us in the girls' changing room, I notice her hair smells of bacon. I've never eaten bacon myself because it's made from pork, which isn't kosher, but I must admit I find the sweet, smoky smell delicious.

I spot Broderick on the blue-and-white tile deck of the pool. He's standing with his hands on his hips. His back and legs are still suntanned.

Isaac has come swimming too. He emerges from the boys' changing room just after Annette, Glynnis, and I come out of the girls' changing room.

"Isaac!" Annette calls out. "You look like a skinny ghost!"

Isaac does look a little ghostlike. A bony, blushing ghost. Though he eats well and has gained weight, he's still thin. Maybe it's because he's so tall. He's hunched over now too—I think he feels embarrassed.

"At least you have a decent bathing suit," Annette tells Isaac. Mom has picked out a pair of navy blue swim trunks for Isaac.

"The ones you girls are wearing look like prisoners' uniforms," Glynnis says. "No wonder they were on sale!"

First, I worry that what Glynnis has said about prisoners' uniforms will upset Isaac. But then, I realize that I should be upset too. She has just insulted our bathing suits—and Mom's taste. I'm about to say something when Glynnis jumps into the pool, her arms stretched out at either side. When her body lands on the water's surface, she splashes so hard we're all covered in fat droplets of water.

"Glynnis!" Annette calls out when Glynnis's head pops out of the water. "You've soaked us!"

"You've come swimming, for goodness sake," Glynnis answers. "Getting soaked is part of the fun!" Glynnis's head disappears back under the water.

"Look," I tell Isaac, "there's Broderick. Do you want to say hello?"

"I have no interest in talking to Broderick," Isaac says. "Besides, he has someone to talk to."

That's when I notice Broderick is talking to Millicent Byrd, the prettiest girl at Westmount High School. Millicent is wearing a shiny black swimsuit, the kind Annette wishes she could have.

"Come for a swim, Rosetta! Don't be a chicken!" Glynnis calls from the pool.

"Go ahead," Annette tells me. "Esther's lesson is over. Isaac and I'll keep an eye on her, won't we, Isaac?"

Two lanes have been roped off for those who want to swim lengths. Just as I'm getting into the pool (I don't bother using the stairs at the shallow end, but I don't jump in the way Glynnis did, either), I see Broderick sail through the air as he dives into one of the lap lanes. Millicent stands by the edge of the pool, applauding.

A lifeguard is keeping watch by the deep end. His sharp whistle pierces the air when he spots two children Esther's age getting too close to the deep end.

Glynnis wants to show me how well she can tread. "You make a scissors motion with your legs," she says, though I haven't asked for instructions.

From the corner of my eye, I see that Annette and Isaac are leading Esther down the blue steps that lead into the shallow end. Esther is trying to splash with her hands, but Annette and Isaac are holding her back, only letting her try to swim a little at a time.

The nice thing about treading is you can talk to your best friend while you do it. And observe other swimmers, like Broderick, who glides like a dolphin through the lap lane.

"Why do you think Millicent isn't swimming?" I ask Glynnis.

"It's either because she wants to show off her bathing suit or because she's on her period." Glynnis disappears under the water after she says that, but I know she's laughing because air bubbles come rising to the surface. Which makes me laugh, too. I dunk my head underwater, and Glynnis and I wave at each other. Everything feels as if it's happening more slowly underwater. Glynnis's blonde hair floats by her ears, mermaid-style. When I come up for air, the sharp smell of chlorine fills my nose, making the tiny hairs inside quiver.

"Tell me what bacon tastes like," I say to Glynnis as the two of us bob up and down.

"Wouldn't that be a sin?" Glynnis's eyes are dancing.

"It'd be a sin for me to eat it; it's not a sin for me to hear about it. So tell me."

"Well, it's crunchy and salty and a little burned."

"A little burned? That sounds awful."

"It isn't. You'd love it if you tried it."

"I won't try it. Ever."

I let myself sink under the water again.

It's when I'm underwater that I notice something's wrong. Every pair of legs I can see from down here—little legs that belong to small children, large sturdy legs that belong to their parents—seem to be shifting, changing their angle. And though I'm underwater, I can feel the panic spreading through the pool, rippling out to where I am.

Glynnis notices something, too, because when our eyes meet, hers have a look in them I've never seen before: fear. And because Glynnis is the most fearsome fearless girl I know, the look in her eyes makes me even more afraid than the panic I sense all around me.

Don't let it be Esther, I think, as I push to the surface, panting.

It isn't Esther.

It's Broderick.

Chapter 25

I know it's Broderick because of the way Millicent is shrieking, "Do something! Someone do something!" from the side of the pool. Later, I will wonder why Millicent didn't do something herself. Even if Glynnis was right, and Millicent is on her period, surely, judging from the way she was talking with Broderick this morning, she would want to try to save him.

I know it's Broderick because all the panic—the arm waving, the rushing of legs, the gasps, and the shouting—are focused on the lap lane Broderick was in.

And I know it's Broderick because when I look around, there's no sign—no sign at all—of his suntanned shoulders.

Glynnis elbows her way past other swimmers.

"Let me by!" she says, and her urgent tone of voice makes the others move away and clear a watery path for her.

I follow Glynnis, like a car following an ambulance as it tries to rush down a narrow street. "What do you think has happened to him?" I ask her.

"A cramp, maybe. I told him not to eat so much!" Glynnis answers fiercely, without turning to look at me.

The lifeguard whistles three times in a row. The piercing sound echoes in my head. "Get out of the way! *Tous*! All of you!" he shouts. But even the lifeguard sounds worried, and I remember what I once read: if a person remains underwater too long, even if he's still breathing, the brain can suffer permanent damage.

What if that is happening to Broderick?

Other swimmers move away from the lap lane so the lifeguard will have room for a rescue. There is a loud splash as he dives into the pool.

Glynnis is swimming so fast now I can't keep up. Besides, I'm having trouble breathing because I'm so upset, and that's making it harder for me to swim. Instead, I tread water the way Glynnis showed me, while I try to catch my breath . . . and watch.

I feel as if I am at the movies, watching a scary film, the kind that makes you grip the armrest.

The lifeguard disappears under the water. Half a minute later, he emerges, with Broderick.

Broderick is flailing his arms, slapping the water. I am close enough now to see the crazed look in his pale blue eyes. And then I watch as Broderick does a terrible thing: using both hands, he grabs hold of the lifeguard's head. The lifeguard tries to fight him off, but fails. The lifeguard gasps and then disappears back underneath the water.

What is Broderick thinking? Is he so desperate for life that he's willing to risk the safety of the lifeguard who has come to his rescue? It doesn't make any sense! Now Broderick is sinking back down too. It's his eyes I notice most. They are glued to the ceiling, like a frog's. It's as if he thinks looking up will help lift him from the water.

"Brod—!" Glynnis calls out, her voice breaking.

Now I see Isaac, standing at the edge of the pool, exactly where the lifeguard was when he dove in. My eyes dart over to the stairs. Where's Esther? But now I spot Esther clinging to Annette the way a baby monkey hangs on to his monkey mother. Annette is trying to cover Esther's eyes, but Esther—being

Esther—is peeking out from under the safety of Annette's elbow.

Isaac dives into the water. "Who is that boy?" I hear strange voices ask.

"A war refugee," someone whispers back.

"He seems to know his way around a pool."

"Thank goodness for that."

Now three heads emerge from the water at once: Broderick's, the lifeguard's, and Isaac's. Broderick must have swallowed a lot of water because he is sputtering like mad. The lifeguard tries to say something to Broderick, but from where I am I can't make out the words. But I know from the look on the lifeguard's face he is trying to calm Broderick down.

Isaac is several feet behind Broderick now, out of his view. A moment later, there's another giant splash. At first, I think someone else has dived into the pool. The splash is followed by an almost animal yelp of pain. From Broderick. His face is gray, and his pale blue eyes have turned to ice.

It's only later that we learn what happened beneath the water's surface: Isaac has kicked Broderick—hard—in the back of his legs. "With all my strength," Isaac will explain that night, over dinner. "And to be honest, I enjoyed *myzelf*."

The kick was part of Isaac's plan. He had seen what was happening to Broderick, that he was panicking and becoming dangerously aggressive. The kick was meant to startle him.

It also buys Isaac time, because just when Broderick is yelping with the pain of being kicked, Isaac swims up to him and grabs his arms, pinning them behind his back. Broderick won't be able to grab for anyone's head now.

Together with the lifeguard, Isaac, swimming backward, hauls Broderick from the pool and drags him out onto the tile deck. Broderick's chest heaves as he coughs up water.

"Let me by! Let me by!" I hear Glynnis say as she struggles to reach the side of the pool.

I watch spellbound as Isaac perches over Broderick's body and with his fist, pumps down hard—three times—on Broderick's chest. More water comes spurting out of Broderick's mouth. But Broderick's eyes are closed. His eyelids do not flutter.

Millicent is standing nearby, her hand over her mouth.

Isaac lifts Broderick's left arm over his head. The arm flops down on the deck. Lifeless.

"He's unconscious," the lifeguard shouts. "Someone find a doctor! *Un médecin! Vite!* Quick!"

If only one of the adults in the pool was a doctor, but no one comes forward. What terrible bad luck!

Isaac pushes the lifeguard away. Now Isaac leans again over Broderick's body and presses his lips down on Broderick's. Isaac breathes deeply into Broderick's mouth. Once and then again. I'm reminded of the passage in the Book of Genesis where God gives Adam life by breathing into his lungs. The breath of creation. Then Isaac pumps hard again on Broderick's chest.

Glynnis has climbed out of the pool. She's hunched over Broderick too; her eyes are glued to his face. "He's opening his eyes!" she calls out, and it's as if, at that moment, everyone in the pool or standing on the deck sighs with relief. As if we've all been holding our breath and have now, finally, exhaled together.

Broderick is still on his back, his head propped up by a towel someone has folded and tossed over to Isaac and the lifeguard. "Tell us your name," the lifeguard shouts at Broderick.

"Brod, Brod—" He is too weak to get the whole name out. But at least he can speak. If his brain was damaged, surely he would not be able to form words.

"And the year?"

"1942."

"Broderick," the lifeguard says, "you just had a very close call."

Broderick nods.

"I believe you owe your life to this man." The lifeguard lifts his eyes toward Isaac.

"Thank you," Broderick says. His eyes are still focused on the ceiling. Just the effort of these few words seems to have exhausted him, and now he shuts his eyes.

"Broderick!" Isaac's voice is so loud Broderick opens his eyes again.

What Isaac says next comes out much more quietly. Only Broderick and those of us who are nearby can hear it. "How does it feel," Isaac asks, "to know you owe your life to a Jew?"

Chapter 26

You can imagine how grateful the Benbows are to Isaac. They insist on stopping by after dinner. Mrs. Benbow has baked shortbread with the last of the family's weekly ration of sugar. She starts to cry when she hands Isaac the tin of cookies; Mr. Benbow can't stop shaking Isaac's hand. "You're a fine young man," he tells Isaac. "The very finest. I want you to know that I'm going to do everything in my power—everything—to see you are accepted into the McGill Faculty of Medicine. That a fine young man like yourself would be kept on some waiting list makes no sense. No sense at all!"

Is it my imagination, or does Mr. Benbow repeat everything he says?

Mom and Mrs. Benbow are sitting together on

the small blue velvet settee, having tea. Mom puts her cup down on the end table. "We believe the reason why Isaac is on the waiting list has something to do with"—Mom pauses—"his religion." Mom and Dad exchange a quick look. "Our religion," Mom adds.

Mr. Benbow does something I have never seen him do before: he blushes. Then he takes a white linen handkerchief out of his pocket and uses it to dab at his forehead. "These quotas that we're being asked to observe make things very difficult. But Isaac deserves to get in. Despite his . . . your . . . religion." This time, Mr. Benbow doesn't repeat any of his words.

Dad gets up from his armchair by the fire, and for a moment, I worry he's about to smack Mr. Benbow. What will happen to my friendship with Glynnis, then?

Mom gets up now, too, and rests her hand—firmly—on Dad's forearm.

"I hope you're not saying you agree with these quotas," Dad says to Mr. Benbow.

"Why, no, of course not." Mr. Benbow dabs at his forehead again. "And of course, it isn't only Jews who are"—Mr. Benbow stops to choose the next word—"affected . . . by the university's quota system. It's women too."

If this is Mr. Benbow's plan to improve relations with my parents, it isn't working. Mom marches over to him. "If I was a member of your blasted admissions committee," (I have never heard Mom use the word *blasted* before) she says, looking him straight in the eye, "I'd make sure we accepted the very best candidates . . . no matter their race or religion . . . or gender! And may I add my fervent hope that one day, McGill University will graduate more female doctors than male ones!"

This time, Dad rests his hand firmly on Mom's forearm. "I'm afraid we're all getting a little too excited here. It's been a big day for all of us. The Benbows nearly lost their son." Mrs. Benbow sniffles loudly when Dad says this. "And our Isaac managed to save the day. Gerald's already said he'll do whatever he can to see that Isaac gets into McGill's Faculty of Medicine. And I even think—if I may say—that he is beginning to see the foolishness of this quota system. So, I'd say that, together, we have much to celebrate." Dad lifts his cup and saucer from the table. "And so, I'd like to propose a toast to Isaac, our future doctor, and to a world where people are judged on their merit and not, as Irene has said, on their race, religion, or gender. So, to Isaac, and to equality for all men and women!" Dad's eyes meet Mom's, and they exchange a smile.

"Hear! Hear!" Mr. Benbow says, reaching for his cup and saucer, too, and clinking them against Dad's. Mom and Mrs. Benbow do the same. Then everyone insists on clinking teacups with Isaac and saying again what a fine young man he is.

I'm the last one to toast Isaac. "Here's to you," I say, "Dr. Guttman."

* * *

Mom and Dad haven't breathed a word about Mom's visit to the eye specialist last week. When they got home from the appointment, Dad was holding Mom's hand. I heard Annette asking what the doctor had to say and then Dad's terse answer: "Things aren't yet clear." At the time, I didn't see the irony behind Dad's words, though I don't think he was trying to be ironic. For Mom, things are getting less and less clear as her eyesight worsens.

I've been too busy considering my public

speaking career and then Isaac's heroics to give much thought to Mom's eye trouble, but tonight, when I am brushing my teeth, I overhear Mom and Dad talking about it. They are whispering, my cue that this is a conversation worth eavesdropping on.

"I don't want to burden the girls. Not now," Mom says. "They have enough on their minds. I think they're still adjusting to Isaac's presence."

"Irene," Dad says, "I think it's important you have their support. Your condition," Dad lowers his voice even further when he says this word, "is going to mean you'll be relying on them and me more and more. You'll need us to be your eyes."

I nearly cry out when Dad says that. *You'll need us to be your eyes.* So Mom really is going blind! How terrible! And what about the specialist in New York? Can't he do something to restore Mom's vision?

"It's the writing I worry about most," Mom says. I'm surprised by how calm she sounds. If it were me—and what if I've inherited Mom's condition the way she inherited it from *her* mother?—I'd panic. Just the thought of never seeing all the things I love—the orange berries on the mountain ash, the view of the city from the lookout at Mount Royal . . . and what about books? How can a person read if she can't see? Why, I'd go crazy!

"The girls will help you with your writing . . . you can dictate your poems to them," Dad says gently. "Annette will want to do it. But I think Rosetta would do a better job. Of all our girls, she's the storyteller. A nuisance, sometimes, I'll grant you that, but a storyteller."

I'm devastated at the thought that Mom may not regain her vision, and I don't like being called a nuisance (and by my own dad!), but I must admit I do feel proud when Dad calls me the storyteller in our family.

"Rosetta will be your amanuensis."

I don't know what *amanuensis* means, but I like the sound of it. A lot.

* * *

Because it's Sunday night and Anne-Marie is off, Isaac and I are on dishes duty. I wash; he dries. Every once in a while, he hands me back a plate or a glass. "If you weren't in such a hurry, Rosetta," he says, "you'd do a better job."

"Maybe you're too fussy. Or maybe my eyes

aren't as good as yours." I bite my lip when I say it. Am I already beginning to lose my eyesight?

I've made myself so upset that one of the plates slips out of my hands and falls into the ceramic sink, breaking into long, jagged pieces. Isaac stops me when I reach down to collect the shards. "You'll cut yourself," he warns. "Wait for me."

Isaac disappears and returns with the first section of yesterday's *Gazette*. There's the article I read announcing that Queen Juliana, the Dutch queen who moved to Ottawa after the war broke out, is expecting a baby. The Dutch royal family is asking that instead of sending gifts well-wishers make a direct contribution to the war effort. It's awfully noble of them.

I step out of the way, and Isaac reaches into the sink, using the newspaper to protect his fingers as he collects the shards.

"Mom'll be terribly upset. These plates were a wedding gift from Granny."

"We can glue the plate back together."

"It'll look awful."

"You know what my Tante Dora used to say?" It is the first time in ages Isaac has mentioned Tante Dora.

"What?"

"That broken things that are glued back together are the most beautiful of all."

"Did she say that after something broke?"

Isaac nods. "Yes, she said it when I broke one of her precious Meissen bisque figurines. I accidentally knocked it off the shelf with my fishing rod."

"Maybe she was just trying to make you feel better."

We work in silence for a while. I try to do a better job scrubbing so Isaac won't make remarks.

"I'm worried about Mom," I say as I rub at a stubborn spot of dried-up mashed potato.

"She'll forgive you for breaking the plate."

"It isn't that." I hand Isaac another plate.

He examines it before wiping it dry. "What is it, then?"

"She really is going blind. I heard her and Dad talking before. There isn't anything the eye specialist can do. Oh, Isaac, just imagine what a sad life she'll have—she won't be able to see a thing!" I don't mean to cry, but I do.

I'm expecting Isaac to hand me the dish towel to dry my cheeks or say something kind, but he doesn't.

"At least you have a mother!" His tone is harsh. As if he doesn't have any sympathy for me at all.

I turn to face him. "I do have a mother," I tell him. "And so do you! Just because you can't forgive her for the things she's done doesn't mean she's dead."

"She's dead to me," Isaac whispers.

"But she isn't really dead, is she, Isaac? Dead people don't send letters, do they?" I think about what Miss Vipond told me. "Did you ever consider the possibility that your mother might not be a complete monster?"

"She is," Isaac's voice is muffled, "a complete monster."

"It's easier to tell yourself that, isn't it?"

"Easier than what?"

"Easier than trying to understand why she did the things she did. Why she gave you up. And taught at that *Mädchen's* school." I know what I'm saying is hurtful, but I feel like I'm lancing a wound. Trying to release the liquid festering inside. And I'm not finished. "You know what, Isaac?"

"What?"

"You like your wounds!"

"What are you talking about?"

"You wrote that in your letter to me. You meant to write *I lick my wounds*, but instead you wrote *I like my wounds*. I think it's true! You do like your wounds."

Isaac storms out of the kitchen.

I'm left to dry the last of the dishes on my own.

I'm not sorry I said what I did. Not even a little bit sorry.

Chapter 27

Isaac isn't the only one who's upset with me. So is Annette. I borrowed her white blouse to wear to school (it's true I didn't ask her permission, but if I had, she'd only have said no) and I got the tiniest speck of cement glue on one sleeve. Anne-Marie tried to wash it out, but she couldn't, so now there's a minuscule gray fleck on the left sleeve.

Of course, Eagle Eyes noticed it straightaway. "I will never ever let you borrow anything of mine again!" she shrieked. "Do you hear me?"

"Of course I hear you. You are yelling like a banshee," I say, covering my ears. "Besides," I add, "It's too small for you."

"That's not the point! You can't be trusted. That's the point, Rosetta!"

I tried explaining that it happened when I was

gluing together Mom's plate, but Annette didn't care, not even when I told her broken things that are glued back together are the most beautiful of all. "Who told you that rubbish?" she asked, rolling her eyes.

Mom's not too pleased with me, either. "I know it's not the end of the world, dear, but I did rather like having a complete set of dinner dishes." At least Mom was a little more open to the idea of repaired things being especially beautiful. "I see the point," she told me, "though I think it applies more to people than plates."

Esther is downstairs playing checkers with Anne-Marie. Since I haven't anything better to do, I decide I might as well work on my speech. Though I haven't told anyone yet—not even Glynnis or Miss Vipond—I've decided not to give up on my public speaking career. My cheeks still get hot when I remember how everyone giggled when Mom's underpants were caught on the back of my tunic, but I know now there are much worse things in the world than that. Take, for example, Mom's going blind or everything that has happened to Isaac—not to mention everything that is still happening across the ocean.

I haven't decided upon the topic for my new speech. I want it to be something more important than breakfast. But what? And that's when it occurs to me. I can do a speech about Isaac and what it's been like for all of us to finally have a brother. I could even work in something about how Isaac saved Broderick from drowning! The audience will love that part!

I bring my writing block and pencil downstairs to begin my interviewing. I don't want to make the whole speech about me.

Esther advances one of her checkers. "What would you say it's been like having Isaac for a brother?" I ask her. My pencil is in position to record her answer.

"It's all right," she says, "for now."

The *for now* part makes Anne-Marie laugh.

"Why are you writing notes?" Anne-Marie asks.

"I'm thinking of doing a speech about what it's been like to have a ready-made brother."

"You should ask Isaac's permission before you make a speech about him," Anne-Marie says.

I don't want to admit that Isaac is ignoring me again. "I don't see why I need his permission. It's my story. Our story," I say, correcting myself quickly.

Esther sighs. I think it's because she is losing at checkers. "It's Isaac's story too," she says.

Annette is coming downstairs.

"What do you have to say about having Isaac for a brother?" I ask her.

"It took some getting used to, but now I like having him for a brother. What I don't like is having to share my room—or my blouses—with the likes of you!"

★ ★ ★

Dad is at Mom's desk, doing the accounts for our synagogue. His ledger book is open, and he has a pencil tucked behind one ear. I want to speak to him, but I'm afraid to interrupt while he is calculating. He must feel me hovering. "Ronald," he says, "do you have something to tell me, dear?" The way he asks makes me think he doesn't mind my interrupting him. When he turns to look at me, he rubs the skin beneath his eyes. For a moment, I can imagine what he'll look like when he is old.

"It's about Mom's plate," I say. "The one I broke."

"Oh that," he says. "I think she's gotten over the loss."

"What I wanted to ask you is, Do you think Birks might sell those plates? If they do, I could save up and buy her a new one."

"I think it's a splendid idea, Ronald. It just so happens that I've got a meeting later this week near Phillips Square. I'll stop in at Birks and see about the plates. I wouldn't be surprised if they carried them. Now why don't you plant a kiss on my old cheek, and after that I'll get back to my numbers?"

★ ★ ★

I'm still not convinced I need Isaac's permission to do a speech about what it's like to have a ready-made brother. Then I try reversing the situation in my head. How would I feel if Isaac did a speech about having me for a ready-made sister? I wouldn't like it very much. And I'd want to know about it first!

So I decide to speak to Isaac. Besides, I want to try to patch things up with him.

I knock on the door to his room. I think it's the first time I've thought of it as Isaac's room and not mine. Though I know he's in there, Isaac doesn't answer.

"Isaac! It's Rosetta. I've come to ask you something."

Still no answer.

I knock.

"I thought we weren't speaking," he says at last.

"Well, you're speaking and I'm speaking, so I suppose that means we *are* speaking." I try to keep my voice light. I don't want Isaac to know how much I want to be friends with him again.

"Don't you ever just give up, Rosetta?" Isaac asks from behind the door.

"Never. I never give up. Ever. It's on the Wolfson family crest."

"It is?"

"If it isn't, it should be."

The door cracks open. On the floor, I see the strip of fabric with the yellow stars, but I decide not to say anything about it.

"I'm sorry if I upset you last night. I was just . . ."

"Trying to help," Isaac says, finishing my sentence. At first, I think he's teasing me, but then Isaac pats my hand. "I'm sorry myself. I'm worried about your mother's eyes too. It's just . . . sometimes, I think I get a little jealous. I shouldn't have gotten so angry. You don't deserve it. It's my mother I'm angry with. And maybe you're right. Maybe I do like my wounds. Did I really write that in my letter?"

"You did."

I fight the urge to tell Isaac again that he might be wrong about his mother. I don't want to risk upsetting him all over again. Besides, maybe, just maybe, Isaac could be right about his mother. Maybe she is a monster and he is better off treating her as if she's dead. Maybe I am not always right.

"You said there was something you had to ask me?"

"So you forgive me"—my eyes drift down to the strip of fabric on the floor—"for everything?"

"I do."

The inside of my throat suddenly feels thick, and for a moment, it's hard to swallow. "Would you mind very much, Isaac, if I did my public speaking speech on what it's been like having you for a brother?"

I expect Isaac to answer straightaway, Isaac-style, but he doesn't. "I don't mind, as long as you don't tell just the good parts or just the bad parts, either. Do you understand what I mean by that, Rosetta?"

"That was my plan exactly."

Chapter 28

Anne-Marie has offered to iron my hair. She's more cheerful than usual. I think it's because her family has had a letter from Jean-Claude– a short one, but still a letter. From what they can tell (all letters from prisoners of war are censored), Jean-Claude seems to be all right. The main thing, Anne-Marie says, is that he is alive, unlike so many of the boys who were at Dieppe.

"Dinner's made," Anne-Marie says. "The house is dusted. And because I've just finished ironing all your father's shirts, the iron is hot. Besides, this way you'll have straight hair for your speech on Friday."

When Anne-Marie mentions my speech, I know it is her way of making things up to me for the underpants incident.

I am leaning my head back on the ironing board—most uncomfortable!—and Anne-Marie is ironing my hair. She has put a towel between the iron and my hair so the ends won't get burned.

Afterward, my sisters—even Annette—say my hair looks lovely, but the person I really want to show it to is Glynnis. So I rush up the street to her house. Broderick answers the door. He has finally lost his summer tan and looks as pasty as the rest of us. "You look different," he says to me, "more grown-up."

"Anne-Marie straightened my hair. I wanted Glynnis to see it. Is she home?"

Glynnis must hear my voice because she has come to the top of the staircase.

Even without his tan, Broderick is still handsome. But somehow, not handsome to me anymore. Maybe to Millicent and to every other girl in Westmount, but not to me. I think it's because I don't just see him—his hair, his face—I see more. I've seen parts of Broderick that aren't handsome at all.

Glynnis likes my hair. "But don't let a drop of moisture touch it or it'll frizz up like a dandelion again," she warns, shaking her head.

The doorbell rings and, of all people, it's Isaac. He looks a little frantic, and I worry that something's wrong at home. "Did you come to see Broderick?" Glynnis asks him.

"No, not at all. I need Rosetta. Right away, please."

Isaac seems not to realize I'm standing in the hallway, just behind Glynnis.

Glynnis thinks this is hilarious. "You mean you don't recognize your own sister? It must be on account of her new hairstyle."

Isaac's dark eyes seem to double in size. "Is that you?" he asks, a little nervously. "You don't look like yourself."

"Is everything all right at home?" I ask Isaac.

"Yes, yes, everything's fine. But I just had a phone call from Mrs. Etkowitz at the Canadian Jewish Congress. It seems her daughter, that friend of yours—Bertha—mentioned my situation. Mrs. Etkowitz told me Mr. Bronfman wants to meet me. Today. She says there's news on Tante Dora's file. I asked if I could bring you along, and she said yes. But we need to leave immediately. Will you come, Rosetta?"

"How exciting! Of course, I'll come. How kind of Bertha to tell her mother about you."

"Do you mean that awful girl you know from synagogue?" Glynnis asks.

"For the record," I tell Glynnis. "She isn't awful."

"Well, then," Glynnis says, "let me get you a head scarf to protect your hairdo."

"I haven't time," I tell her as I pull on my coat.

★★★

Mrs. Etkowitz is not wearing one of her feathered hats. She kisses me on both cheeks, shakes Isaac's hand, and then brings us into Mr. Bronfman's office. It's a great honor for us to meet him. Mr. Bronfman is, after all, the president of the Canadian Jewish Congress, not to mention one of the wealthiest men in all Canada. The Bronfman family owns the Seagram Company. People say the Bronfmans made their fortune selling bootleg whisky during the American Prohibition, but I decide it's better not to mention that.

Mr. Bronfman extends his hand to shake Isaac's and mine. "You must call me Mr. Sam. Everyone does. And let me say it's a great pleasure to meet you." Mr. Bronfman has even less hair than Dad. He is wearing a well-cut suit. Behind his eyeglasses, he has sharp, intelligent eyes.

He directs us to two leather club chairs and takes a seat behind his desk, which has a glass top. "My friend, Mr. Schwartzberg," he says, "has told me a little about you, and frankly, I should have looked you up by now, Isaac. And you, too, Rosetta. I've met your parents, so I wasn't surprised to learn that they—you—have opened your home to Isaac. Is it true, young man, that you've been accepted into the Faculty of Medicine at McGill University?"

Isaac flushes. "Well, not exactly. You see I'm on the waiting list, but from what I understand, my name's been moved up."

"That's because Isaac's a hero," I can't help interrupting.

"A hero? Indeed? Mr. Schwartzberg didn't mention that part of the story."

Isaac gives me a sharp look, but he can't stop me from telling all this to Mr. Bronfman. "Isaac saved Broderick Benbow from drowning. At the Westmount YMCA. He performed mouth-to-mouth resuscitation. I was there!"

"Remarkable," Mr. Bronfman says.

I hear Isaac take a deep breath. "I believe you have news for me about my aunt. Dora Guttman."

"I like that you take a businesslike approach to things, young Isaac," Mr. Bronfman says. "As for you," Mr. Bronfman looks over at me, "I like your spirit. You remind me a little of my wife, Saidye. She founded the Women's Division of the Combined Jewish Appeal, and she's got all four of our children knitting blankets for the boys overseas."

There's a stack of manila file folders on Mr. Bronfman's desk, and he reaches for the one at the top. He opens the file and glances at the first page inside it. "I'm sorry it took us so long to get this information," he tells Isaac. "But you know better than any of us how"—he stops to choose his next words—"chaotic things are in Europe nowadays. And frankly, young man, you confused us when you said your aunt paid for your passage on the Kindertransport from Germany to Britain."

"But she did," Isaac says.

"She did not," Mr. Bronfman says. His voice is firm, but not unkind. "According to our affiliates in Britain, thanks to the Nazis, your aunt was, unfortunately, penniless. It was someone else who paid to get you on that Kindertransport." Mr. Bronfman consults the sheet of paper in front of him and points to a typewritten name. I try to read it upside down, which is hard to do.

"Ulrike Knopf. I hope I'm pronouncing it correctly." Mr. Bronfman and I are both watching Isaac's face.

Isaac covers his mouth with his hand. "That can't be," he says, his voice so quiet I have to strain to hear him. "Ulrike Knopf is my mother."

"Well, then," Mr. Bronfman says, "that makes perfect sense. I understand you've already been informed about your Tante Dora's death, which happened during one of the Nazi transports. May I offer my most sincere condolences? But we're pleased to inform you that your mother appears still to be alive and well. It did strike us as rather odd that you hadn't inquired about her status. Would you like us to try and make contact with her on your behalf?"

"She . . . she . . . is a supporter of the Nazis," Isaac says. He is pressing the heels of his hands into his eyes. I know it's because he doesn't want to cry.

Mr. Bronfman leans back in his chair as if this will help him make sense of what Isaac has just told him. "Is she?" he asks. "Because even if she is, it looks to me as if she went not only to considerable expense but also that she must have put herself in considerable danger—especially if it's true that she had ties to the Nazi Party—to ensure your safety. Like it or not, young man, it's thanks to her you were able to leave Nazi Germany."

Chapter 29

So much for straight hair. Even with the fire blazing downstairs, the house is damper than a dishrag. Outside, it's drizzling. Anne-Marie gives me a sideways look when I sit down for breakfast. "Shall I iron it one more time before you go?"

"No, it'll only frizz up again. Besides, it's a waste of electricity."

My legs shake as I take my place behind the podium. I know everyone in the auditorium is remembering the underpants incident. And though I had planned to begin my speech by telling about Isaac straightaway, I decide at the very last moment to begin with something else. Because I know Glynnis will disapprove of any changes, I make a point of not looking at her.

"Ladies and gentlemen, I used to think the worst

thing—the very worst thing—that could happen to a person was to do a speech without realizing her Mom's underpants were stuck to the back of her tunic." Everyone in the audience laughs, and all the awkwardness I was feeling—and maybe also the awkwardness the audience was feeling too—seeps out of the auditorium like air from a balloon.

When I resume my speech, I can feel how everyone is focused on me, the me who is in front of them right now. Besides, I'm not the same me I was that day. Which is exactly what my speech is about. Though I have notes, I don't need them. What I have to say doesn't come from the *Britannica*; it comes from inside of me.

"I don't think that anymore. My thinking changed when, about two months ago, our family expanded to include a ready-made brother. Until then, we were five: my parents, my two sisters, and me. But now there's also Isaac. And it's Isaac who is responsible for the change in my thinking that I was telling you about just now. Isaac is a refugee from the war going on across the ocean. If he hadn't managed to get out of Germany on something called a Kindertransport, he would almost certainly have been murdered by the Nazis."

People shift in their seats when I use the word *murdered*, but I don't let that stop me. I don't care if my speech is difficult to listen to; I don't even care whether or not I win today's competition. I just want to make my audience understand.

"You see," I continue without bothering to read off my sheet, "like me, Isaac is a Jew. And for no good reason, Hitler and his Nazi Party want to destroy the Jewish people, not only in Europe"—I pause for effect—"but throughout the world."

"We must do everything we can to stop Hitler and the Nazis." I look up at Glynnis. She gives me an encouraging nod and signals that I still have five minutes left.

"The stories I'm about to share with you are harrowing, and you will need courage to hear them. Do you have that kind of courage?" This time, when I pause, I look out at the audience. Several children nod, and one or two call out, "Go ahead and tell us."

So I begin telling them about what has been happening in Nazi Germany: how when the Nazis first came to power, Jewish youngsters like Isaac were forbidden to attend school and how his Tante Dora's business and possessions were confiscated and about how children learn hatred at school. I tell them how German Jews are forced to wear the yellow star with the word *Jude* in it. I also tell them how Tante Dora died on the cattle car. And about Mr. Schwartzberg's family.

"The newspapers tell us about the battles our brave Canadian troops have been fighting, but we hear little about what is happening to Europe's Jews. It was not easy for Isaac to share his story, but I think you'll agree that it's important and that it's a story we all need to know so we can do our part."

"You see, I'm here today to tell you about brotherhood. Not just brotherhood in the sense of having a brother, the only boy in a house with three sisters. Not just brotherhood in the sense of having to share the bathroom with one more person, a person who does not always remember to lower the toilet seat." The audience laughs and I join in. I think we all needed a little comic relief.

Glynnis signals that I have four more minutes. "I mean brotherhood in the broadest sense. That we are all brothers and sisters" (I think about my sisters when I say this, but especially about Annette. I know I need to try harder to get along with her. Otherwise, my speech will be a lie, and I don't want that) "no matter our race or religion or beliefs. That we need to look out for each other and be kind to each other and stand up, whenever necessary, for each other and against injustice. We must also do our part to insist that the government of Canada allows more war refugees into our beautiful country, and we must welcome these refugees into our homes and our hearts."

Just then, the door to the gymnasium cracks opens and I see Isaac. I am so glad to see him that for a moment I forget all about my speech. Seeing my reaction, the audience turns too. Now we're all looking at Isaac.

"That's him! Isaac! I recognize him from the YMCA," one of the teachers calls out.

Someone claps. Someone else, probably Gerald O'Shaughnessy, whistles.

Isaac has a cardboard box in his arms. I know exactly which box it is.

I invented a new beginning to my speech, and now I feel a new ending coming too.

Isaac looks at me, and we exchange a nod. Without words, I have asked a question and he has given me his answer.

Yes.

"I'd like all of you to meet my ready-made brother, Isaac Guttman."

Isaac blushes, but then he takes a little bow. "Good afternoon," he says.

"Isaac has brought something to show you. It's a kind of proof of what's been happening in Europe. He's going to show you some of those yellow stars I just told you about. The ones with the word *Jude* on them. The ones German Jews are forced to wear so they can be identified as Jews—and mistreated for nothing more than being Jewish."

Isaac is walking through the aisles, showing the students the cloth stars. Some of the children want to touch the orange-yellow fabric, and Isaac lets them.

The auditorium has gone very quiet.

Glynnis signals that I have less than a minute left for my speech.

"Try to imagine being forced to wear one of those yellow stars on your clothing," I tell the audience.

Isaac is showing the stars to every single person in the auditorium. The teachers want to see them too. Miss Vipond reaches out to touch them. I've never seen her look so solemn.

I clear my throat. "I want to thank all of you, but

especially Isaac." He doesn't look up when I say his name. But I know he is listening.

"Thank you, Isaac"—I'm afraid my voice will break—"for sharing your story with me, for letting me share it with my friends, and for being my brother."

Now the audience claps so loudly the whole auditorium vibrates.

I don't know exactly how it happens, but later, on our way home, I end up carrying Isaac's box and he ends up carrying my trophy. Miss Vipond said that I could take it home for the weekend to show my parents, but I'll have to bring the trophy back on Monday so that it can go to the engraver.

"It was an excellent speech," Glynnis says.

I'm so surprised by her comment that I stop in my tracks. "Don't you have any criticisms at all?" I ask her.

Glynnis's blue eyes twinkle. "Maybe something will come to me later."

Glynnis wants to stop at our house on her way home.

"Shoes! Shoes!" Anne-Marie calls from upstairs when she hears the three of us come in.

But we've all taken off our shoes, even Isaac.

Dad is home early from the office. We join him, Mom, and Esther in the parlor, where they are having tea. Annette and Anne-Marie come downstairs to join our impromptu party.

"What can I do to help?" Anne-Marie asks Mom.

"Just sit down and have a cup of tea," Mom tells her.

Everyone wants to know about Isaac's trophy. "It's Rosetta's. She took first place in the public speaking competition."

"How wonderful!" Mom and Dad say at the same time.

"But Isaac deserves some of the credit," Glynnis says. "He brought along some of those orange-yellow fabric stars the Jews in Germany are forced to wear. The judges give extra points for visual aids."

Mom turns to look at Dad. I can tell from the way she's raised her eyebrows that she is concerned about something.

Dad pats Isaac's elbow. "Is everything all right, Son?" he asks.

"Rosetta," Mom says to me, "I hope you didn't push Isaac into doing anything he wasn't ready for."

"Mom."

We're all surprised to hear Isaac call her Mom. Annette nearly chokes on her tea.

"And Dad."

For the first time, there's nothing awkward in the way Isaac says Dad.

"Rosetta didn't force me into anything. But if I contributed in some small way to Rosetta's success, I'm glad. After all, that's what brothers are for."

I could never have imagined a brand-new brother would appear on our doorstep. But now, I can't imagine our house without Isaac in it. Though we may not always get along, Isaac is my brother. He's not so brand-new anymore– he's just my brother.

ABOUT THE AUTHOR

Monique Polak is a regular contributor to the *Montreal Gazette* and has been published in many other major publications. She lives in Montreal with her husband and daughter, where she teaches writing and English literature.